FORGING HALCYON

Paperback ISBN: 979-8-9923338-0-0
E PUB ISBN: 979-8-9923338-1-7

Cover art by Manu

Book & Cover Design by Eugene Pendley
Printed by Ingram Spark
First Printing, 2024 Edition

Published by Merchants of the Void

www.eugenependley.com

FORGING HALCYON

EUGENE PENDLEY

CONTENTS

To My Dearest Feral Cousin,
Krista Smith

This story wouldn't exist without you

CHAPTER 1

A Simple Country Smith

The song of metal striking metal shot through the air, the rhythmic ring piercing the hazy air of the smithy and beyond. One calloused hand held the red hot nail in place with thick calipers while the other wielded the heavy hammer in perfect time to shape it. The smith paused to carefully inspect it as the metal cooled under his watchful eyes. Satisfied, he dunked it in a bucket of water with a hiss, then tossed it into a nearby bin with many others. Distant shouting from outside intruded on his mind, but he dismissed the sound with a grunt. He placed the next length of steel into the fire and worked the twin bellows to raise the heat to hellish temperatures. As the flames flared, he told himself the voices from town were none of his concern.

"You there, smith!" a voice from the open wall of his shop called, cutting off his thoughts.

His eyes glanced up, though his hands did not stop, and eyed the dirty ruffian that darkened his door. With a curt nod, he returned his gaze to the bellows.

"Boss needs a bridle ring repaired," the ruffian said as he tossed a worn and broken metal ring on the nearby bench. "Now," he added boldly.

The smith glanced at the worn and dirty metal for a heartbeat, then returned to the fire. "One silver for a new ring. The tanner can finish the repair for you," he quoted.

"A silver? You must be a bit thick, old man. You're going to give us the ring or I'm gonna come back with some guys to convince you," the ruffian said, taking a bold step forward.

The smith's face remained unchanged as he removed the glowing nail from the coals and picked up the hammer. The anvil sang again as he hammered the metal into shape with perfect rhythm.

Like the last, he inspected it, dunked it, and tossed it into the bin.

"Do your ears work, old man?" the ruffian said.

The smith took a step towards him and pointed to the broken ring with the heavy hammer, his actions smooth and casual. Soot and sweat smeared his face like war paint, but his eyes were clear as crystal as he held the intruder's stare. The smith's threat hung heavy in the silence, outweighing the ruffian's words.

"It's a fortnight's ride to the nearest smith who can fix that bridle, in good weather at that," the smith said, his voice hard but calm. "You can tell your boss if he offers me so much as a rude word, he can ride his boot heels the whole way there for his bridle and every horseshoe he needs for the rest of his days." He dropped the hammer onto the bench with a thud and picked up the broken ring. "A silver is an honest price for honest work. The metal is decent, so I'll give you half a silver in trade for it. You can pay in coin or boot leather, your choice."

The ruffian stared at him hotly for a long moment, but the smith was unmoved. Finally, the man produced a small pouch with an irritated sound and handed him several small coins. The smith counted them, then tossed the broken ring into a large bin partially filled with scrap metal. He rummaged through a second bin and produced a similar-looking metal ring which he tossed to the ruffian.

"There you are," he said conversationally. "Take that to the tanner, and he should be able to fix up the bridle quick enough."

The ruffian inspected the ring, then turned to leave.

"One more thing," the smith said as he retrieved his hammer from the bench. "If any misfortune finds the tanner, you'll not find honest prices at my shop ever again."

The ruffian met his eyes briefly but then left without further argument. The smith tread to the back of the shop and dropped the coins onto the rough wood table. As he took a long swallow of clear water from a tankard, crunching footsteps approached on the gravel outside. He scowled as he left his tankard and met the visitor in the front. Instead of the ruffian, a tall man shrouded in a well-kept cloak met his eyes instead.

"I assume you are the one known as Eggar, yes?" the man said in a clear voice.

"I am," Eggar replied.

"I am here to pick up a brooch commissioned some time ago. I was told it was ready?"

Eggar inspected the man and his plain but expensive clothing. He was most likely a wealthy man from the city trying to avoid unwanted attention on the road. Considering the growing number of local bandits, it was a wise choice.

"It is," Eggar said. "Let me fetch it for you. You have the payment, I assume?"

"I do. Happily so, unlike some of your patrons," the man said, his voice rising as Eggar walked out of sight into the back of the shop.

Eggar chuffed a laugh. "The local bandits like to test me sometimes, but I'm not shy when showing them where the mark lies."

Eggar glanced over his shoulder to ensure his guest couldn't see, then removed a small wall section that concealed a metal strongbox. He retrieved a small bundle wrapped in cloth, then sealed the hiding spot once more.

"Is it wise to antagonize them?" his customer asked as Eggar rejoined him.

"I'm the only smith in the region, and no other would consider opening a shop as long as those pests remain," Eggar explained. "The younger ones are equally ignorant and arrogant, but their leader is no fool. He knows how much he needs me."

Eggar unwrapped the cloth bundle and handed the customer a silver brooch bearing a delicately crafted moon and stars. The customer's eyes lit up as he handled the piece, inspecting each meticulous detail.

"This is marvelous work, Eggar!" the customer complimented. "A friend claimed you to be a brilliant smith, but I admit I had my doubts until this moment. I mean no offense," he quickly added.

"None was taken," Eggar said casually. "It's true that most of my work is in nails, horseshoes, and the odd plowshare. It is rare that I get to work with such fine metals. Best keep that out of sight, though. If the brigands see it, I'm sure they wouldn't hesitate to relieve you of it. A wealthy man traveling alone might want to avoid attention anyway, bandits or not."

"I am simply here to retrieve your work for my master," the man said with a warm smile as he handed over a pouch of coins.

"If you say so, sir," Eggar said with a nod. "Servants in these parts don't typically have such well-tended clothes, nor are they quite so well spoken. By the way you hold my work and the look in your eyes, I'd also wager that brooch holds personal meaning to you. I am but a simple country smith, though. Perhaps I'm wrong."

His customer laughed softly. "It appears I am caught. I am as much a servant as you are a 'simple country smith' though," he said. "You have quite the eye for details."

"The craft requires it," Eggar said as he counted the coins in the pouch. "There are those among the brigands with equally sharp eyes, so take care." With a small scowl, he handed the coin pouch back to his customer. "This is far beyond my price, sir. I cannot accept."

"The quality is far beyond my expectations, so it is a fair exchange. I insist," the man said with a grin. "Besides, if what you say is true about the brigands, it may be in safer hands with you."

Eggar laughed and accepted the coins with a thankful nod. "It is appreciated, and my family will be thankful for it."

"You have a family?" the man asked as he stowed the wrapped brooch securely under his cloak.

"I do," Eggar said proudly. "A wife, a son, and a daughter."

"You are blessed indeed," the customer said with a wide smile. "I hope I am half as blessed after my wedding."

Eggar's eyebrows lifted in silent question.

"The brooch is a wedding present for my-" the customer said but caught himself. "My soon-to-be wife," he finished. "We first met under a clear night sky and spent the night marveling at the moon and stars."

Eggar nodded with a happy smile. "To be young and in love. It appears you have two blessings already, but I wish you many more," Eggar said as he motioned his guest outside, away from the dust and smoke that lingered.

"Have you ever considered moving into the city? You could work for the Lord himself with your skills, and your family would live free of these bandits."

Eggar shook his head. "It is a nice thought, but these people would suffer without me. They need a man who can work metal, but I also give them some protection from the bandits. Even if that were not the case, the few times I have visited the city, I found the air thick and the streets crowded. Here the air is sweet and the paths spacious."

"That it is," the young man said appreciatively. "Have you considered petitioning the Lord for help with the bandits, at the least?"

"The villagers have on a few occasions, but it seems our problems are but small ones for our Lord," Eggar said as he watched the band of brigands ride from town with a cart full of ill-gotten goods.

"Really?" the young man asked, a pained and contemplative expression on his face. "I have some dealings with the local Lord, and I shall bring the issue before him the next we meet."

Eggar glanced at his guest and sensed he withheld something, but also that he meant what he said. "I would be glad of such kindness, no matter the outcome."

The customer nodded once, then set his eyes on the village below. "Well, I must go if I am to make any meaningful ground by sunset. It is a comfort to see the brigands ride east as I head west."

"There are many more than what you see here, good sir. Be wary in your travels," Eggar said as he held out his calloused palm.

"Always," the young man said as he shook Eggar's hand firmly. As the young man made his way down the gravel road toward the village, he turned and waved. "It was very nice to meet you, Eggar!" he called.

"A pleasure to meet you too, sir," Eggar called back with a warm smile.

He stood in the sun and watched the man walk for a long moment, enjoying the gentle breeze. With a scratch of his beard, he marched to his desk and deposited his day's wages in the hidden strongbox. After a short break, the rhythmic song of metal on metal resumed.

CHAPTER 2

The Ones We Love

The pale morning sun lit the way for Eggar as he walked down the dirt road into the village with the small bundle of food his wife had prepared. It was unpaved but well traveled, so the earth under his feet was packed and fairly even. The weather had been dry, and he was thankful there were few muddy spots to slow him down. The tall grass on each side of the road grew into a living wall this time of year, often high enough to block sight lines and muffle sounds. Despite the danger their slender bodies could hide, he appreciated the moments of peace in a day ruled by fire and noise. The rustling of something approaching quickly broke him from his thoughts as his heart leapt in his chest. A boy, maybe eight or ten years old, burst from the grass and gave the burly smith jump terribly.

"Boy!" Eggar exclaimed more hotly than he intended "You about startled me to death! What are you doing lurking about in the grass?"

"Bandits!" the boy said with an ashen face as he sucked in fresh air. "They attacked the village and I ran into the grass. I got lost and thought I'd never find my way out!"

"The bandits attacked?" Eggar asked, alarmed. "Is anyone hurt?"

"I know not, sir," the poor boy said breathlessly.

"Come, let us make haste," Eggar said as he broke into a run with the boy close behind.

When he reached the village, the situation was not as bad as he anticipated. There were no shouts of violence, nor smoke from burning rooftops. The only sign of something wrong was a knot of townspeople huddled around something on the ground. He broke through the ring of people and saw a badly beaten man in the dirt. A young woman kneeled beside him, fretting about his wounds but not knowing how to help. It was the tanner's daughter, he knew her well.

"Eggar, please help my father!" she cried as soon as she saw him.

He bent down and assessed his friend's wounds as best he could, only barely recognizing him. They were grievous and beyond his meager ability to help, but perhaps he could keep the man alive long enough for more able help to arrive. He looked into the crowd and saw the boy from the grass.

"Boy, fetch the healer. Fast as you can!" he ordered.

"Right away, sir!" the boy said and disappeared into the crowd.

Eggar turned back to his friend on the ground. His face was badly bruised and swollen, his clothes torn in several places. A large gash across his chest worried him most. It was not wide but appeared deep and oozed blood constantly at one end. Again, he searched the crowd until his eyes met two large men he recognized from the fields.

"You two, help me lift him and carry him to his house," he said, then turned his attention to the daughter. "Run ahead and clear the dining table for us, then fetch some clean rags. Quickly dear!" he exclaimed when she remained frozen in place.

His words snapped her to action, and she ran toward the nearby house. Eggar and the two men lifted the tanner as gently as they could, trying to ignore his pained cries. The short journey felt like eternity, but they eventually made it inside the humble home. The heavy dining table was bare, and the daughter rushed in with an armful of clean cloth. The men laid the tanner on the table as gently as they could and Eggar used a rag to put pressure on the bleeding gash, much to the tanner's discomfort.

Eggar met the eyes of one of the men that accompanied him. "Go outside and watch for the healer," he said, his voice tightly controlled but calm. "Send him this way as soon as you see him, and keep any onlookers out. The last thing we need is idle hands crowded around."

The muscular man nodded and left.

"What happened?" Eggar asked the remaining field hand.

"The bandits returned demanding their usual 'tribute,' but there was not much to give," he explained.

"So soon? They were here, what? Two days past?" Eggar said, his anger clear.

The man gave a curt nod. "One of the bandits suggested they take the daughter in trade for the missing payment, which Elias wasn't going to stand for. A fight broke out and then a bunch of the other bandits joined in. They beat him something awful. I guess you can tell that much."

"Only fists?" Eggar asked.

"Fists and feet," the man said solemnly.

"I supposed that's a good thing," he said.

He checked the bandage, but blood began to seep out as soon as he lifted the cloth. It had pooled on the tabletop, and threatened to drip onto the floor. He scanned the room for something, anything, to help. He was glad to see a low fire burning in the hearth but dreaded what must come next.

"Dear, do you have a poker for the fire or some other thick bit of metal?" Eggar asked the daughter.

She nodded but did not remove her eyes from her wounded father.

"Fetch it and place it in the fire, then stoke the flames as high as you can."

Again she nodded distantly, but despite her shock, she left her father's side to do as the smith had asked.

"Do you see anything he can bite down on?" Eggar asked the man.

"Would this work?" the man asked as he handed him a thick wooden spoon.

Eggar nodded and set it on the table next to Elias. He watched the fire and the handle of the poker sticking out closely, judging the heat. Time ticked by as the flames grew and Eggar silently prayed for his friend.

"Bring the poker here, girl," Eggar said to the daughter when it was ready, then turned to the man. "Hold him down, no matter how hard he tries to fight you."

The daughter brought the dimly glowing poker to him as the man braced Elias' shoulders firmly. Eggar took the poker and removed the bandage once more.

"I'm sorry about this, friend," Eggar said, bracing himself as he placed the spoon handle in his friend's mouth.

He pressed the hot metal onto the seeping wound and Elias immediately returned to full consciousness. The air in the tight quarters filled with muffled screams and a nauseating smell as the metal hissed. Elias stopped thrashing and went limp on the table, which in turn sent his daughter into a panic.

"Is he dead?" she asked, terrified.

Eggar shook his head as he removed the poker and handed it to the daughter. "No, he's passed out. Put this back in the fire for me. We shouldn't need it again, but best to be prepared."

Eggar inspected the wound. It was blackened and horrible looking, but it wasn't bleeding. His friend's breath was shallow and ragged, but steady. There was nothing more to do but wait on the healer, so he sat heavily on one of the rough stools beside the table. The three waited in grim silence until the door opened and an old man in robes entered. He went immediately to Elias' side and inspected the injuries with practiced efficiency.

"This burn here was not from the fight, I take it?" the healer asked.

"No, that was my doing," Eggar said. "The wound would not stop bleeding, so I burned it shut."

"Quite effectively done. Where did you learn such a thing?" the healer asked.

"Working up at the smithy, I am familiar with cuts and hot metal," he explained.

The healer grunted in reply without taking his eyes away from his patient. "Well, there is much yet to do. I thank you both for your work here, but I'm sure you have other matters to attend to."

Eggar met the daughter's eyes once more before he turned to leave. "If you need anything, come see me."

She nodded in reply and offered a weak smile. "Thank you, Eggar. For everything."

Eggar ran the edge of the sickle blade along the grinding stone as glowing sparks flew into the dimly lit shop. It was late, and he would normally be putting things in place to head home for the night, but the morning's events had put him behind schedule. Even if it hadn't, he didn't feel like going home. He had spent most of the day beating his anger into glowing metal or working the bellows as the coals flared with his pain. Having let his anger burn out, his soul felt scorched and empty. He didn't want to bring that home to his family, so instead, he sat and refined the edge of a blade that had been sharp for some time.

"Evening, friend," said a voice from the darkness outside.

Eggar's heart jumped, but the only outward sign was a slight flinch.

"Apologies, I didn't mean to give you a fright," the voice said as a cloaked and hooded man walked into the candlelight.

The man was of average height but heavily framed. His clothes were worn and patched, bearing the dust of long travels. His back was slightly bent but his movements were smooth and steady. He would have assumed he was a wandering trader, but he carried no goods or signs of the wealth that came with it. The stranger scanned the shop idly and gently touched some tools hanging on the wall.

"Quite alright," Eggar said as he stood and stored the sickle blade. "What brings you to my shop so late?"

"I was passing by and saw a light," the stranger said. "I was curious what troubles would keep a talented smith toiling in the night." The stranger shifted his gaze from the hanging tools to Eggar's eyes. "Bandits, perhaps?"

The light from the nearby lantern spilled under his hood as he turned. He was old enough to be an elder in most villages. The locks of hair that rested on his forehead and the stubbly growth on his face were both more gray than not. The deep wrinkles of his skin, however, were not thin and papery like most old men, but leathery from wind and sun. The age apparent in his face was not reflected in his eyes. They were clear and keen, gazing at the world around him but also through it.

"It is late, stranger. Who are you, and what do you want?" Eggar asked, his anger stirring languidly beneath the surface.

"I am but a wanderer," the stranger said, ignoring the tone. "I travel from place to place, observing the world's workings and collecting knowledge. Occasionally, I see an opportunity to..." the stranger trailed off as he gazed around the shop, searching the walls for the words he wanted. "To correct an imbalance," he finally said. "That is what brings me to your shop this wonderful evening."

Eggar stood and watched the stranger with a stony face.

"I hear you are a man of great talent when it comes to shaping metal, and I just so happen to possess the design for a powerful weapon," the stranger said as he removed a bound scroll from beneath his cloak. "A weapon that could easily defend your village from any sort of bandit or brigand. A weapon that could bring peace to you and yours."

"What exorbitant price do you want for such designs?" Eggar asked flatly, familiar with his type and wanting no part in his schemes.

"Price? No, you misunderstand. I ask no payment," the stranger said with a seemingly genuine smile.

"I am old enough to know the price is heaviest when the seller claims there is none," Eggar said as he turned away to straighten his tools. "I am not interested, and you can be on your way, good sir."

"Your hesitance is most wise; I would probably do the same," the stranger said as he returned the scroll to its hiding place. "I will be in town for three more nights, no more. Should you change your mind, place a mark on the door to your shop, and I will return," he said. He placed a stubby bit of white chalk on the table by the door, then met the smith's eyes. "Three nights, Eggar. Do not wait too long."

With that, the stranger melted into the night, and Eggar was alone once more.

CHAPTER 3

Loss

The next day, Eggar kept himself busy around the shop. He tried not to think about his injured friend or the mysterious visitor, but instead buried his mind in his work. There was always something to do, even on days like this when his stocks were full and no orders waited. Instead of working metal, he focused on the ever neglected task of organizing and cleaning.

If that was not enough, he could spend some time with his pet project: A special forge in the cave behind his shop. After years of construction and adjustments, it was finally functional. With some fine tuning and a little luck, he might be able to reach temperatures that could fully melt the sturdiest metals. Perhaps he could even create alloys never seen before. He idly leaned against the heavy support beam of his shop as he wistfully gazed toward the cave. The calipers he'd been cleaning nearly dropped from his hand, which snapped him out of his daydreams. He shook his head and smiled, feeling silly for entertaining such grand aspirations. It would probably never work, but maybe he could use it to melt down ore and reforge scrap more efficiently, saving him time and coin. A knock on the wall behind him drew his attention, and he turned to see the exhausted healer.

"What can I do for you today, good sir?" Eggar said, his dreams fading away. "Do your blades need sharpening so soon?"

"No, they remain sharp as ever," the healer said, his voice heavy. "I'm afraid I come with the burden of ill news. Elias the tanner has passed away, victim to his wounds."

"How could this be?" Eggar asked as he sat heavily on a nearby stool, the shock of the healer's words sapping his strength. "His wounds were grievous, but he seemed as if he would pull through."

"I suspect the cause was something deeper and hidden from the eye," the healer said gravely. "He woke long enough to speak with his daughter and take last writes before his passing, which is some comfort."

"That it is," Eggar said, his mind reeling.

"Elias was a good man, always fair and honorable in our dealings, and I heard nothing different from anyone else in the village. I know you two were close, so I felt I should bring word myself."

"Thank you, I appreciate that," Eggar said softly. "What of his daughter? Where is she to go now?"

"She has family nearby that will take her in until she comes of age, and arrangements are already being made. I suspect she will depart in the morning for hopefully brighter times," the healer said, his eyes distant. "I must return to my duties, but do you need anything while I am here?"

Eggar shook his head, but then met the old man's eyes. "Tell his daughter if she needs anything before she departs, of me or my family, she has only to ask."

The old healer nodded to him with a smile, then turned back down the road to the village.

Eggar sat on the stool for a long while, his sadness turning to anger once more. The bandits had first been a nuisance, then a hardship to be borne, but now they had taken his friend. They had taken a father from his child. They would continue to worsen until someone stopped them. The villagers had traveled to the city several times to plead for help from their Lord. Each time there had been hope, but never action. Only empty promises. Someone needed to do something before more people died. The village was on its own, but who among them could stand against armed bandits?

His anger soured into black despair as he hung the nearly forgotten calipers on the wall. Lost, he plodded to the door and spied the bit of chalk the stranger had left, still on the table where the hooded man had left it. The stranger had promised a weapon that could give the village the means to defend itself. It was probably a ploy for coin (or he was insane) but no harm could come from looking. He was an experienced smith and could spot a worthless design. He wouldn't hand over any coin unless it was good. At worst, he would waste a moment of his time. If the plans were true, perhaps he could prevent one of the villagers from sharing the fate of his friend. Even a slim chance was worth a look, right?

He picked up the chalk, locked up his shop, and drew a long slash across the closed door. There were no projects to take on, and he was no longer in the mood to putter about. He turned his back on the smithy and walked the road home. His normal route took him through the village, but this afternoon he chose one that would take him around the outskirts instead. He did not want to talk to anyone or hear their condolences. He just wanted to get home and see his wife and kids. Perhaps their smiling faces could drag his mind away from the day's dark news, even if only for a while.

The road home was long and empty, with only the grass and a gentle breeze to keep him company. Thoughts of bandits, weapons, and lost friends drifted from a sharp pain to a dull ache. He wondered if the mark on his door had been a mistake, an act born from the pain of loss and the heat of frustration. He was too far home to turn back, but he could erase the mark come morning. If the stranger showed, he would send him on his way again. His mind was clear when the grass gave way to his yard and house. He hesitated at his door as he looked over his shoulder toward the village and his shop, then opened the door and headed inside.

"Eggar, you're home early today, dear," his wife said with a surprised smile.

He replied with an affirmative grunt and set the remains of that day's lunch bundle by the door. "A slow day," he said as he sat in his usual chair. The house was quiet and empty today. "Where are the children?"

"Alexander is out tending to the horses and seeing about the cart," his wife said as she returned to mending one of his shirts. "Kat went with him. You know how she follows her brother around like a shadow these days."

"It's good for her to learn about his chores. I know it's considered man's work, but if she is to run a household one day, she'll be glad of it. What is wrong with the cart?" Eggar asked.

"The harness again," his wife said. "The straps are getting old, and one broke. We should see Elias about a new one soon, once he recovers."

The reminder of his friend was like a slap in the face and he turned his sour expression to the fire.

"What is it Egg? You look ill," she said as she set her needlework down.

"The healer paid me a visit at the shop today," he said heavily.

Her lovely face fell, dreading whatever came next.

"Elias passed some time in the night from his wounds," he said as he fought back the pain.

Her hand covered her mouth in shock, and she joined his gaze into the fire. "That is terrible news, he was a good man. Oh, and his daughter..."

"She has family nearby who will take her in," Eggar said.

"That at least is a blessing," she said sadly, then laid a gentle hand on her husband's arm. "How are you love? He was a friend to us both, but you have known Elias for ages."

"I'm okay," he said as he met her eyes.

Her simple beauty always struck him, and the compassion in her eyes now only accentuated it. Her long dark hair was pulled back in a familiar knot, which nearly matched her dark brown eyes. Her skin was tanned and freckled from working in the sun, not at all like the porcelain skin of noble ladies. She would be dismissed as common stock by those of higher birth, but Eggar deeply appreciated her fortitude, both of body and of spirit.

"It pains me something terrible, but I will survive," he added.

She gave his arm an encouraging squeeze, then returned to her needlework. "It is news we may need to get used to hearing, unfortunately," she said with a frown.

"Why is that?" he asked, breaking away from his thoughts.

"Our neighbor came to visit this morning, just after you left, bearing news of the bandits. It seems their recent return was due to trouble shortly after their previous visit. Talk is, one of their hideouts was raided and they lost the a large store of goods."

"Joyous news," Eggar said, enjoying the thought of them being preyed upon for a change.

"That is what I thought too," she said, meeting his eyes briefly. "Our neighbor pointed out that they will get more aggressive as they grow desperate from the losses, should they continue."

Eggar grunted with understanding.

"Also, there was no word on who routed them. Perhaps the Lord has finally seen fit to act against such brigands, but perhaps a worse band has set their eyes on their territory instead."

"A dark thought indeed," Eggar said.

"She was worried about her family, but I told her there was little danger. We are close to the village but removed from the main roads. I doubt bandits would waste the ride to bother a handful of humble cottages."

That had saved them trouble in the past, but Eggar suspected if they became desperate enough it would matter little. His position as smith would matter less as well if thoughts of their future dimmed. In such circumstances, being removed from the village would only put distance between them and help. If bandits occupied the village, their cottages on the outskirts would be the best place for retreating brigands to hide should they be routed, at the peril of whoever lived there. At the peril of his family. His thoughts turned back to the stranger and the promise of a weapon.

"Are you alright, love," his wife asked. "You seem miles away. I didn't mean to add to your burdens."

"No, I'm glad you told me," he said with a shake of the head. "My thoughts had returned to work, is all."

"In the shadow of bandits and woe, my husband thinks of metal and hammers," she teased.

Eggar chuckled and smiled at her warmly, but it faded quickly. "It has been ages since I have forged a sword, but I was thinking of making one for Alexander tomorrow."

"Is that wise?" she asked, slightly alarmed.

No official mandate prevented the common folk from bearing arms, but the nobility generally saw it as a sign of brewing rebellion. A good sword was also easy to sell, for a good price, which in turn invited violent people to relieve their owners of them for quick coin.

"I'm familiar with how to swing a sword and could teach him too, at least enough to defend against these untrained imbeciles. Should they try to flee in our direction, he or I could at least attempt to defend our home," he explained.

"I see your point, but what would the Lord think of you making swords for commoners?" she asked.

"It would only be the one and it wouldn't be questioned if the son of a smith owned one," he said. "If questions arise, we could claim he wants to train to become a soldier one day. That I do not think they would take offense to."

"Oh, perish the thought of our son becoming a soldier!" she said with wide eyes. "I fret at the thought of him defending our home, much less riding off to some rich man's war."

"Agreed," Eggar said gravely.

His wife sat still for a long moment considering their situation. "I think it would be a good idea. If danger is likely to find us, we should prepare as best we can."

Eggar nodded in agreement as his heart warmed for her. She bore dark times and hardships with such poise that it seemed easy, something he both marveled at and envied.

"I think I hear the kids approaching. Let us leave thoughts of battles and blades in favor of brighter days," she said, her face content and kind.

"Gladly," he said, pushing away the storm clouds in his mind.

He heard the distant crystal laugh of a young girl. The sound was marvelously happy and poured warm sunlight into his soul. He knew it would not be a challenge to enjoy this evening with his family. It never was.

Eggar sat his small bundle of food in the back room of the smithy as his mind churned through the day's tasks, despite his worries. It was early and sleep slowed his thoughts, but familiar labors promised a fine distraction. A knock on the large shop door drew his attention.

"Who on earth..." he asked himself as he lumbered toward the sound, hoping it was not more bad news.

He unfastened the thick bolt and swung the wide door outward, prepared to lash it to the wall like usual but froze at the sight on the other side. The stranger from the other night was standing still as stone with a small, satisfied smile. The morning sun did nothing to dispel the unusual air that Eggar had assumed was lantern light and tired eyes.

"Good morning, Eggar," the stranger said happily.

"Morning," Eggar conceded, not enjoying the sound of his name coming out of the man's mouth.

"You have changed your mind about the weapon?" the stranger asked, his face neutral but his eyes keen.

"I agree to nothing until I have seen the plans and you detail the exact cost of such a thing," Eggar said sternly.

"I ask no price, good man, but let us examine the design and go from there," the stranger said without offense.

Eggar waved him inside as he opened the door and secured it. The morning air was still crisp, so he would wait until the forge was lit before opening its twin on the other side. The stranger had unfurled the pages on the nearby table and weighed the corners with a handful of thick nails from the bin. Eggar bent over the table and examined the oxidized markings on the yellowed pages. There were many notes in a language he did not recognize, but the illustrations were meticulous and clear.

"This is for a scythe, not a weapon," Eggar said with a frown, wondering if the man truly was mad.

"Ah, but it only appears as such," the stranger said with a wide smile. "See here? This mechanism allows the blade to be folded for storage or swung to a vertical orientation."

"I see, much like a polearm but with a significantly longer blade..." he said. "This locking mechanism is quite clever, but how is it used?"

The stranger pointed to a small drawing at the bottom of the page.

"Ah, a concealed lever in the handle," he muttered admiringly. "With that placement, the wielder could easily modify the blade's position in combat. Theoretically, someone could wield this as staff, scythe, and polearm as needed. There are several flaws, however"

"Oh? What do you see," the stranger asked, his expression curious.

"The locking mechanism is clever, but in a fully extended position would be a point of weakness when the blade struck. A reinforcing bracket could be added here," Eggar said, pointing to the parchment. "The blade could lock into place against it. If the bracket were to extend down the length of the shaft, the lock would bear almost no weight from the heaviest of strikes."

"If the handle were metal, you could shape that in, could you not?" the stranger asked, impressed.

"Certainly, but a wooden handle would allow it to be hidden away and transported with mundane tools. Defending the village would best be done without inviting too much attention, lest there be rumors of brewing revolt."

"Quite wise," the stranger said.

"The other problem is the balance," Eggar pointed out. "A blade of such size thick enough to fight with would be incredibly heavy, and all toward the top. A thinner blade would help, but would break easily."

"That is not a problem," the stranger said, meeting his eyes. "The design calls for a special alloy considerably lighter than steel and unbreakable when completed."

"All blades can be broken," Eggar said, voice full of doubt.

"No force in this world could break this blade," the stranger said seriously.

Eggar stared into the stranger's eyes for a long moment and saw no hint of madness or deception, but remained skeptical.

"Well, with lighter metal I could make the back end of the blade slightly thicker than what is shown here and taper evenly into the cutting edge. When folded, the thicker spine would be beneficial for striking anyway. A thin fuller along the spine could also help balance the weight if necessary. Perhaps a counterbalance could be worked into the opposite end of the shaft as well..."

"Shall I take it you're interested?" the stranger asked.

Eggar stood straight, his back cracking as he did. "Not until you explain your interest in forging this blade. Everything carries a cost, and I will not consider this until I know what it is."

"I simply want to return balance to your village," the stranger said with honeyed words.

Eggar stared at him flatly.

"Fine," the stranger said as his face fell. A look of muted bitterness replaced the facade, one finally reflected in his eyes. "Let us just say I am at odds with a group, and the forging of this blade would be quite the insult. I simply cannot pass up such an opportunity. They sit back and watch the world's pain, afraid to interfere lest they accidentally make it better. By helping you, I gleefully spit in their eye, even if they never realize it."

"What happens to us when they come seeking retribution?" Eggar asked, concerned.

The stranger laughed, the sound genuinely amused. "My dear smith, ages will pass before they so much as take note, and kingdoms would turn to dust before they took action. If they ever did. Besides, they will know it was my doing and you only the instrument. A smart man does not curse the tool, but the hand. A wise man knows to curse his own carelessness."

Eggar thought about his words but did not doubt that the stranger meant them. "You truly ask nothing of me and mine in return for this weapon?"

"My vengeance outweighs all the wealth in the King's treasury to me," the stranger said passionately. "To be honest, I care little what happens to the blade once it is forged. Defend the village with it, sell it, or use it to hang your apron. I care not. I only ask that you make it."

Eggar thought for a long moment as he stared at the odd man. He might be mad, but the plans were good.

"Very well. What do we need for your alloy?" Eggar asked.

"Ah," the stranger said with a grimace instead of the joy Eggar expected. "There, we may have a problem. The alloy requires a rare metal, which I know a traveling merchant possesses. Luckily, he is headed into town today, and we can acquire it."

"At what cost?" Eggar asked flatly, seeing the catch after all.

"Oh, that is no matter. I will take care of that," the stranger said without concern. "The problem lies in the metal. It will need to be smelted with immense heat. Much more than your forge could attain, and I know no craftsman capable of it."

"I might have the solution," Eggar said hesitantly. "There is a cave behind my workshop where I have been experimenting with a fixed furnace. With any luck, it should reach higher temperatures than any other."

"Excellent news! Fortune smiles on us, for the required sacrifice has also been delivered to our doorstep. I shall send the merchant your way and make the necessary arrangements for us to acquire the prisoner tonight," the stranger said with a gleam in his eyes.

"Wait," Eggar said, alarmed at the new information. "What sacrifice is needed, and what is this about a prisoner?"

"Have you not heard the news?" the stranger asked, confused. "Oh, of course not! It was only this morning," he added more to himself than the smith. "A small band of soldiers came into the inn this morning speaking of bandits. They were on patrol when they ran into the very ones responsible for the death of your friend. It was a route, and the rogues were captured. They are being held at the old garrison for a couple of days before they travel to their judgment in the city," he said, pointing to the far side of town.

"What is this of a sacrifice then," Eggar asked, noting he had omitted that part.

"The sacrifice," the stranger said as if Eggar should know and became further confused at Eggar's puzzle face. "It is detailed at length in the scroll. Did you not read it fully?"

"It is in a language I have never seen before," Eggar said hotly. "I couldn't read it if I wanted to."

"Ah!" the stranger said, throwing his hands in the air. "I am very sorry, friend! By your understanding of the design, I assumed you could read the words. I wondered how a country smith, skilled as you are, could read such an ancient language." The stranger wiped his hand down his face, thinking. "The design calls for a human sacrifice to enchant the blade once it is forged."

"Oh, no," Eggar said flatly.

The stranger held up his hands, begging Eggar to listen to him for a moment more. "There is a man among the prisoners who is badly injured, he will surely not survive the journey to the city to stand trial. I know one of the men guarding them and can arrange for an opportunity for us to cart him away, undetected. We take him, return here under cover of night, and enchant the blade. Once finished, we return his body to the cell before it is noticed he is missing. In the morning, it will look like he died in his sleep from his wounds, and none will ever be the wiser."

"I will not take a man's life for the sake of some magical nonsense," Eggar said, his voice hard as stone.

"I understand," the stranger said, disappointed. "It is an onerous thing to consider. At the very least, would you forge the blade? I could meet you this evening to help with the smelting. The making and enchanting do not have to be done together, and we would not have time to do both on the same night anyway. I do not want you to come to regret such a decision. At the very least, you could have the finest scythe in the land to cut your grass," he said in weak jest.

Eggar considered it for a moment before answering. "I see no harm in that," Eggar agreed.

"Glad to hear it," the stranger said with a slight smile. "I will see you at dusk tonight, then."

With a curt nod, the stranger turned in a swirl of fabric and left the shop. His smithy seemed empty, only his thoughts left to fill the space. He wondered if he was making a mistake working with the madman. In the end, the temptation of working with an exotic metal and finally testing the limits of his furnace was too good to pass up. The scythe could easily be used to defend his family as planned, and the design was sound. With a shake of the head, he turned his mind back to his work and finished preparing the workshop for the day's labor.

The workload was light, so he spent his time hauling fuel and scrap metal up the short path to the cave, preparing. When the chill of the morning warmed into a pleasant heat, Eggar opened the other side of his shop to allow a cross breeze to flit through. He was busy fiddling with the furnace in the cave when he heard the telltale sounds of a wagon clumping up the path toward the smithy. As he made his way down, he spotted the horse and cart of the traveling merchant through the trees.

"Samuel!" he called as he wiped the sweat from his brow with a dirty rag.

"Eggar! Good to see you!" the portly man called back. He brought the horses to a halt and climbed down from his seat. "You look a mess today, my good fellow," the merchant said as he looked over his customer's clothes.

"I have been working on my furnace," Eggar said with a proud smile.

"Ah, that explains my delivery," Samuel said with a twinkle in his eye. "I have coal and a large bag of odd rocks. A strange man in a cloak paid a good price for them in town and said I should deliver it straight away. Odd as them rocks, he was, but I'm not in the business of turning down coin."

"Nor am I one to turn down free material," Eggar said with a smile.

"How is it?" the merchant asked, squinting toward the cave.

"Headed in the right direction, I think," Eggar said. "Tonight will tell."

The merchant nodded, then made his way to the back of the wagon. "Where do you want these?" he asked.

"Just inside the shop for now," Eggar said as he joined him. "It'll take a few trips to get them to the furnace where I can break it down properly. I wouldn't ask that much of you."

"Much obliged," the merchant said as he pulled a large, lumpy sack to the back of the wagon. "These rocks are light for their size, but that doesn't make them light, if you take my meaning."

Eggar lifted the bag with practiced strength but nearly lost control of it. It was indeed much lighter than he'd expected. He hauled it to the workshop and returned to find the merchant struggling with a tall woven basket, presumably full of coal. Familiar with the routine, Eggar offered to take it from him.

"Ah, thank you, good sir. This poor back just isn't what it once was, you know," Samuel said, mopping his brow with a cloth.

Eggar grunted his agreement and repressed a smile. "Age is cruel to us all," he said, the scripted reply well worn and familiar.

Eggar dumped the coal into the hand cart beside his shop and returned the basket to the merchant. They exchanged the usual pleasantries and news from the road, then said their goodbyes. Alone again, Eggar turned his gaze toward the cave. Nervous energy rolled in his belly at the prospect of working with the mad stranger, but excitement beat in his chest at finally perfecting his endeavor.

CHAPTER 4

Borne of Fire

The sun had barely sunk beneath the horizon as Eggar put the last bits of coal and charcoal mixture into the belly of the furnace. Crunching gravel announced a visitor, but Eggar already knew who the feet belonged to. The hooded stranger melted from the darkness, more ordinary than normal. The mystery that had once shrouded him had largely departed leaving only a part-mad wanderer.

"Is it ready?" the stranger asked.

"As ready as it will be," Eggar replied as he ran a hand through his beard.

"Excellent. I have translated the mixture of ore needed for the alloy," the stranger said with an eager smile as he offered a rolled sheet of paper.

Eggar read over the scrawled notes, hoping there were no more horrific surprises. To his relief, the mixture was only composed of materials he already had on hand in the cave. He added the necessary ores to the bin, then poured the bag of strange ore on top. The ores had been crushed into a sandy texture, but he carefully inspected the stream for any remaining chunks. The new ore was beautiful, dark as night yet glinting with bright flecks that reminded him of the night sky. He mixed the ores with a scoop until the powder was consistent, then poured the bin into the top of the furnace, bolting a cap in place once finished.

"We are ready to light the fire," Eggar said nervously.

The stranger watched him with eager eyes but did not speak.

Eggar carefully arranged the kindling and wood inside the lower portion of the furnace with the coal mixture, then set it alight with a thin dowel. Once the kindling was engulfed, he closed the heavy door and bolted it into place. Ready, he positioned himself at a large set of levers set into a strange mechanism in the back wall.

"How does this contraption work, exactly?" the stranger asked as he examined the forge with his piercing eyes.

"It's quite simple, really," Eggar said proudly. "There is an underground spring deeper in the cave where I have built a waterwheel, of sorts. There is not enough room for a full wheel, so I attached buckets to a large belt. This lever moves the top of the belt into the flow of water and starts the mechanism, which works a set of six bellows to feed a continuous blast of air into the fire chamber. The super-heated air is then forced into the top section with the ore. Once the ore melts, the top cauldron can be tipped to pour into this long trough where it cools into an ingot."

"Clever," the stranger said as he examined the rig. "What do the other levers do?"

"These control the speed of the bellows," Eggar said as he dropped the first lever to start the mechanism.

Resonant mechanical sounds echoed from deep within the cave as if some earthen giant had come to life. A rhythmic thump rose, followed by a steady hiss as the furnace flared to life.

"I've found that too much air blows out the fledgling flames or burns fuel too quickly. Once the fire is steady however, the fuel needs much more air to reach higher temperatures, so I needed a way to manage the speed."

"How do you gauge the heat?" the stranger asked.

"Experience," Eggar said, watching the furnace closely. "The color and quantity of the smoke, the sound of the flames. Not much different than any forge in that manner."

They watched the furnace for a while, then Eggar dropped the second lever. The thump quickened and the hiss increased as the vents at the top of the furnace poured white smoke, then none. The air in the cave began to warm despite the wide and open mouth, but the stranger seemed unbothered. Eggar waited and watched, sweat beading on his brow.

"Here we go," Eggar said nervously, then dropped the third lever.

The thump became a racing heartbeat, the hiss a caged roar. The furnace beamed with energy as the vents glowed with refined flames. The cave was sweltering, but the hot air escaping the mouth of the cave drew cold air from its depths, providing some relief. They waited and watched, but Eggar's instinct told him the furnace was not hot enough, despite reaching its peak.

"We need more heat," the stranger called over the roar, confirming his suspicion. "Allow me," he added with a grave expression.

The stranger cast the cloak from his arms and reached for the side of the hot blast chamber. Eggar yelled at him to stop, but the stranger did not heed him. His palms made contact with the hiss and smoke of burning flesh, but the man did not flinch. Eggar watched in horror and fascination as the man chanted in a strange language. The words became a resonant undertone to the roar of the fire, and Eggar could feel the atmosphere inside the cave respond. He could feel the fire grow as if it were fueled by the strangers intense words.

The stranger's face showed no sign of strain as the fire raged inside the furnace, no sign of discomfort as his flesh surely blackened against the furnace wall. Eggar wondered at a frightening possibility: Perhaps the stranger was not mad at all but truly possessed a power and knowledge he thought impossible. A sharp sound snapped his attention back to the forge, a dissonant note that signaled danger. A second note sounded as a crack appeared along the side of the furnace, bright flame glowing through.

"We must pour now!" Eggar yelled, pointing at the crack.

The stranger followed his gaze and nodded, then quickly backed away from the forge.

Eggar threw the first lever up, and the mechanism wound down, bringing the fire down with it. He quickly moved to the furnace and worked the heavy handle to tip the cauldron. A white hot stream poured from the spout and into the long trough, flames dancing before its advance. The air burned and Eggar had to turn away from the heat, but held fast to the handle until the flow stopped. Once it was done, Eggar and the stranger fled the cave in favor of the cooler night air. Eggar's face was slick with sweat, the neck of his shirt soaked, but the stranger remained comfortable and dry under his heavy clothes.

"Your hands," Eggar said as he fanned his wet shirt to cool himself.

"They are quite fine," the stranger said with a chuckle.

He held them up to show skin untouched by the intense heat. Eggar knew for certain he was no ordinary traveler but something else.

"How did you do that? By all accounts, you should not have hands left, much less ones un-touched by flame. How is it you stoked the fire like that?" Eggar asked.

"Experience," the stranger said with an amused smile. "What must we do now?"

Eggar stared at him for a moment in curious wonder before his mind turned to practical mat-ters. "The metal needs to cool and tomorrow can be worked into its final form in the workshop," Eggar said, glancing toward the damaged furnace.

"The heat in the smaller forge will be enough?" the stranger asked.

"It should be," Eggar said, stroking his beard. "I need only to soften the metal, not melt it as we did tonight. Working it into shape will also help beat the impurities out and give it strength."

"I see," the stranger said, staring into the night. "Have you reached a decision about the enchantment for the blade?"

Eggar followed the stranger's gaze into the cool night air. He had dismissed the idea out of hand thinking the stranger completely mad, but now he had seen the stranger's power with his own eyes. The thought of being responsible for the death of a person was still a high price though, no matter the person's guilt or the benefit of the process.

"What is the purpose of this enchantment of yours?" Eggar asked, seeing no harm in the question at least.

"The material of the blade makes it light, but also provides an ideal vessel for magical energies. The enchantment would be placed inside this vessel making the blade unbreakable and sharp enough to rend any material effortlessly. It would also never dull, chip, or tarnish," the stranger said with a gleam in is eyes. "With such a blade, a single untrained man could stand against a disciplined army and be victorious. Bandits and brigands would have no chance of besting the wielder."

The smith thought for a long moment as he stared into the night. "I am still not comfortable with a human sacrifice, even if it ensures the safety of my family," Eggar finally said, although he could feel doubts in the back of his mind.

"Of course, I fully understand your reticence," the stranger said without judgment. "You'll not need my help shaping the blade or fitting the handle tomorrow, so I shall make arrangements to gain access to the prisoner while you do. If you change your mind, we will have what we need to proceed but if not then we simply part ways."

"I see no harm in that," Eggar said with a nod. "Was the man that killed the tanner one of those captured?" he asked, the thought just occurring to him.

"I wouldn't know who that was, I'm afraid," the stranger said with a glance. "If nothing else, we could see if he was. It would be quite innocent to simply go and look."

Eggar grunted into the night, seeing no flaw in the stranger's reasoning but not comfortable committing one way or the other.

"Well, give it some thought and I shall meet you at your shop just past sundown," the stranger said with a friendly pat on Eggar's shoulder. "I am going to go find a hot bath and a warm bed for the night, and I suggest you do the same. Tomorrow will be a long day no matter your choice, I think."

Without waiting for a reply, the stranger walked into the night and out of sight.

"Perhaps let your wife know you will be working late," his voice said from somewhere in the dark. "No need to worry her, just in case."

"Not a bad idea," he muttered to himself as he listened to the footsteps fade away.

His sweat-dampened shirt grew cold and tendrils of weariness took hold of his body. A hot bath and a good night's sleep suddenly seemed like a marvelous idea. He checked on the cooling metal, but it wouldn't need his attention until morning. He quickly closed up the cave and the workshop, then started his way down the road to home by lantern light. His mind turned over and over the image of the stranger's hands on the hot furnace and the sensation of the inferno that had burned inside the forge and within his chest. It was like nothing he had ever experienced. If he could infuse a blade with that kind of power, he would never need to worry about the safety of his family again.

His body felt heavy and sluggish as he pulled the cave door open, his limbs resistant from lack of sleep. Exhaustion and a good scrub had put him to sleep almost as soon as his head touched the bed, but the events of the previous night roused him early. His normally peaceful walk to the smithy was clouded by a silent debate on whether to enchant the blade or not. He was now confident the stranger could do as he claimed, but the moral dilemma of taking a life haunted him all the more because of it.

The air inside the cave rushed out of the large door as he opened it and the smell of hot metal and scorched dust smacked him in the face like a wave. The steady cross breeze from deep within the cave quickly aired it out while the morning sunlight poured in. Impurities had bubbled to the surface of the long ingot as it cooled leaving a black, rough crust. He touched it with a finger, semi-cautiously, but it was fully cooled. He dragged the calloused pad of his thumb across the pebbly surface to reveal pale blue metal underneath.

Eggar tested the high end of the ingot to see if he would need to beat it loose from the mold, but found it had already separated. He lifted the long ingot free, surprised it was a fraction of the weight he expected. It had occurred to him on his walk that a single ingot of steel that size would be onerously heavy and dreaded transporting this one to the shop below. Such a flaw would need to be fixed before the next smelting. Glad his concerns could wait for another day, he lifted the beam out of the trough and carried it over his shoulder to the smithy.

Once the forge was lit, he heated the beam enough to cut it into workable sections, then beat those into a large lump that would fit in the forge. He spent most of the morning hours heating and folding the hot metal to work out the impurities and marveled at how each pass clarified the pale blue color. While light, the metal resisted the hammer and grew stronger. It made working it a challenge, but it was good news for the blade. By the time he was ready to shape the blade, the alloy was quite beautiful.

Eggar measured out what he needed and set the remainder aside to cool and later store. The metal was unlike anything he'd worked with before, stubborn yet willing to be coaxed into shape. The rhythmic beat of the hammer and the clarion song took his mind off his troubles, and before long he worked with a satisfied smile. As the blade took shape, he stopped to check his work more often and his strokes became lighter, gently nudging the hot metal into position. Satisfied, he stepped back and wiped the sweat from his brow as he admired the nearly finished product.

The blade was thicker at the back than the design called for, but the graceful taper into what would be the cutting edge had felt right. The thick spine would also help with durability and the light metal removed much of the priority on saving weight. Lifting it from the anvil, he swung it gently to and fro, feeling the balance. The long curved blade sliced through the air with heavenly ease, lithe and pale as fresh forged moonlight. He placed it gently on the table by the door and stretched his tired muscles. A glance out of the nearby window revealed an afternoon sun, surprising him with the time. He'd unwittingly worked through lunch. Instead of moving to the grindstone like he had planned, he left the blade on the table and retrieved his wife's bundle instead.

He sat outside and admired the weather as he ate, but his mind kept returning to his work and the new metal. His passion had been stirred after years of mundane work. He loved the usual projects and took great pride in them, but this was something new and challenging. The sounds of children playing in the village below wafted up to him through the clear afternoon air and his mood darkened. Such a happy and innocent sound normally lifted his spirits, but this time it reminded him of the dire importance of his work today. Thoughts of sacrifice and magic intruded once more, lending a sour note to the food and scenery. With a scowl, he decided to accompany the stranger to visit the captives where he would decide on the course of action. When he could lay eyes on the man in question, he would know.

With the decision made, the dark cloud of indecision drifted away leaving him oddly relieved. He sat for a moment to savor the feeling, but the blade called once more. He stood and stretched, ready to put the finishing touches on his project. He spent hours gently working the blade at the grindstone, each pass done with precision and patience. The blade took its final shape ever so slowly, coming to life in his hands. Eventually, the grindstone was too rough an instrument, so he switched to a hand-held sharpening stone to finish the edge. Each careful caress of the cutting edge made the metal sing, the note resonant and beautiful. He lost himself in the process until the sun began to dim and he stopped to light the lamp. The forge had burned down and the shop was quiet as the night took over. He returned to the blade and meticulously worked it with files and abrasives to remove the handful of tool-marks left. Finally, he used a worn rag to clean and oil the blade that now glimmered and shined in the flickering light. He nearly sliced his hand open when a heavy knock sounded at the door.

"Who is it?" he asked, both irritated and disoriented.

"It is me, friend," replied the familiar voice of the stranger.

Eggar put down the blade and let the man in, glancing out into the darkness that had settled without his notice.

"Apologies," Eggar said as the Stranger entered the shop. "I'm afraid I have completely lost track of time today."

"Easy to do, I find," the man said idly. "Oh, Eggar! This is magnificent work my friend!" the man crooned as he inspected the blade. "Your skill was woefully understated. This is truly a thing of beauty."

"Thank you," Eggar said, enjoying the compliment. "It was quite a challenge I admit, but an enjoyable one."

"I am glad to hear it," the stranger said as he gently returned the blade to the table. "Not to ruin such a fulfilling day for you, but have you decided on the other matter?"

"I have," Eggar said as his smile faded away. "I agree we should enchant the blade, and I will accompany you to the captives. I'm still not sure if I can go through with taking a life, but I'll decide once I can look the man in the eye."

"A wise decision," the stranger said. "We must leave right away then. Put this cloak on and secure the shop," he said and tossed a dark bundle of cloth to the smith. "We should be back shortly, but best to be careful."

CHAPTER 5

Light of the Moon

The old rundown garrison building was foreboding during the day, but at night it was much worse. The thick stone walls loomed out of the night and the clinging vines that climbed the walls felt as though they concealed prying eyes. Eggar hugged the dark cloak tight and followed the stranger closely as they made their way around the back of the large structure. They used no torches and Eggar struggled to find his way in the feeble moonlight. The stranger, unsurprisingly, had no such issues. If it weren't for his hushed warnings, Eggar would have fallen several times on the short journey.

"Hold here," the stranger whispered suddenly as he stopped the smith with a weathered hand.

Around the corner, the patch of flickering light of a guard's torch could be seen, but not the man. The stranger raised a cupped hand to his mouth and blew into it, sounding a low whistle. Something about the resonance made Eggar dizzy and buzzed through the inside of his skull, both haunting and uncomfortable. The guard emerged from his post with his torch held high to inspect the night. Eggar was concerned he would head their way, but the armed man's posture was relaxed. He stretched, yawned, and then finally walked away.

"Where is he going? Did you cast a spell on the man?" Eggar asked, mystified.

"What?" the stranger asked, confused. "No," he added with a chuckle. "I bribed him earlier and that was the signal. He will make his rounds slowly, giving us time to get in and out. Come now."

Eggar felt silly but followed the man in silence to where the guard had been. A crude stool sat in the small alcove before a thick wooden door. The stranger led the way in and down a series of recently cleaned but run-down corridors into the belly of the garrison. He had delivered materials several times to maintenance crews on this part of the garrison and recognized the path leading down to the prison cells. He had cast some of the heavy iron bars himself, though he hadn't been the one to install them. He started to head that way, but the stranger stopped him with a hand.

"This way," the stranger whispered. "The man we are after is held in one of the garrison quarters."

"Not in the dungeon?" Eggar asked.

"No," the stranger said. "His wounds are too grievous for him to escape, so they have him in a room more suited for the healer's purposes."

"I see," Eggar said, and followed the hooded man.

They eventually arrived at a closed but un-locked door. Inside, the room was largely empty save for a bucket of water, a table with clean ban-dages, and an old bed. Laying on the bed was a horribly beaten man wrapped in dirty, bloodied rags. The style of the clothes was certainly that of the bandits, though the face was far too swollen and damaged for Eggar to recognize. The man's breath came in long, rattling draws. Occasionally a pained moan would escape his sleeping lips. Eggar inspected the man and knew in his heart he could not take this man's life. Even if it would save his family and village.

"Do you recognize him?" the stranger asked from the door.

"I'm not sure," Eggar whispered back, afraid of waking the man and sounding an alarm.

"It would be difficult to recognize anyone in his state," the stranger muttered. "Do not worry about waking him, the healer has him on some concoction to keep him in a deep sleep. Such kindness is wasted on a scoundrel like him if you ask me."

Eggar leaned in close, encouraged by the stranger's words, and noticed a glint of something hidden in the man's rags. Curious, he gently worked to uncover the keepsake.

"From what I have overheard, he and his men were guarding a large cache of stolen goods and a few prisoners. When they heard the soldiers coming, they killed the prisoners and tried to flee with whatever they could carry. I doubt they planned on keeping them alive in the long run anyway," the stranger said idly as he ran a finger across the table.

Eggar slowly extracted the glinting object and to his horror recognized his own work. In his hand was the brooch he'd made for the kind wealthy man who had visited his shop not days before. The man said he was to be married soon.

"You said the bandits killed all the prisoners? Were there no survivors?" Eggar asked, feeling sickness and burning anger spread through his chest.

"No, all the prisoners were dead or too injured to save by the time the soldiers found them."

"How were they killed?" Eggar asked, the anger turning to rage.

"I'm not sure," the stranger said, curious.

"I made this brooch for a very nice man recently. It was a gift for his wife-to-be," Eggar said as he fought to keep his emotions out of his voice. "This man might be the very one who killed him. He could be one of the men who killed the tanner too."

"Even if he isn't, he rode with those that did. Now he will live out the rest of his days in a prison cell, a luxury denied to his victims. Hardly seems fair. Well, provided he survives of course," the stranger said conversationally. "Come, we must go.

Time grows short and the guard will be returning soon."

"Help me lift him," Eggar said, his mind made up. "This man's penance is not yet paid."

Together, they hauled the unconscious man from the rickety wooden cart they'd borrowed to the long workbench inside the shop. Eggar had doubted their course of action with every moan the bandit made on the way back, but the weight of the silver brooch in his pocket kept his resolve from wavering. He quickly lit the shop and bolted the doors and windows, just in case someone were to get curious about the light this late at night. The stranger retrieved the blade and quietly stared at the injured man, an unreadable expression on his face.

"What now?" Eggar asked.

"Now I shall imbue you with the power necessary to enchant the blade. Then it is simply a matter of moving through the ritual," the stranger said, meeting his eyes.

"I must do it?" Eggar asked, the near panic in his voice evident. "I assumed you would be the one to do the magic."

"No need to worry, friend," the stranger said with an easy smile. "Follow my instructions and you'll do fine. It is true that I possess the knowledge and power, but in shaping the blade you are intimately familiar with it. In this instance, your experience far outweighs mine."

"I see," Eggar replied uncomfortably.

"I will be right beside you the entire time and it will only take a few minutes to complete. Once we start though, there is no turning back. Do you wish to proceed?"

Doubt flitted through Eggar's mind, but only for an instant. He had come too far to turn back. The stranger claimed this was the point of no return, but in truth, it already lay behind him.

"Let us be done with this," Eggar said, his tone one of finality.

"Very well, give me your hands," the stranger said, his face devoid of emotion.

Eggar placed his hands inside the stranger's tight grip. At once, he felt a current of energy flow from the stranger into himself. The sensation was intense and disorienting, but not painful. He heard hundreds of whispering voices conversing in his head as his eyes watered, blurring his vision. Just when he feared he would burst, the stranger let go of his hands and the flow stopped. Something inside him felt close to splitting with energy, but it slowly subsided. It felt as if the energy shrank to fit the space, or the space grew to fit the energy. Which it was, he was not sure. He squeezed his eyes shut to clear them, but he still sensed every detail of the shop around him.

"We need to create a link between the man and the blade," the stranger said, his voice heard both in Eggar's mind and ears simultaneously. "Take this knife and cut the man's hand, just enough to get a handful of blood."

Eggar opened his eyes and took the small knife the stranger held, then held the blade to the man's hand. He watched himself slide the knife in a short line. His hands felt as if they belonged to someone else. He glanced at the man's face, feeling guilty, but the man didn't notice the new wound.

"Take the blood and apply it to the blade to be enchanted," the stranger instructed. "Take care not to cut yourself. If your blood mixes, it will bind you to the blade as well."

Eggar wiped the welled blood free of the man's hand, smearing it onto his own. Memories of the tanner's blood seeping through his fingers sprang to mind, but this time he could feel the pulsing energy of life in it. If this was how the stranger experienced the world, it was no wonder his eyes seemed to peer through everything. With great care, he applied the bandit's blood to the blade. Every sensation hummed inside his head, the vibration rattling his soul.

"Close your eyes now, and focus on your surroundings," the stranger said inside his head.

Unable to speak, he nodded his head and closed his eyes. The room went dark, but not his sight. He could feel the stranger, the prisoner, the walls, the individual flecks of dust in the air.

"It's too much," he said, his voice weak and raspy.

"Feel the blade and the prisoner," the stranger said. "Concentrate."

Eggar could feel both clearly, and when he tried to focus on them the room shifted with his attention. The rest of his workshop melted away as all the energy within him stretched a glowing line between the two points.

"Excellent," the stranger said, either aloud or in his mind. He couldn't tell anymore. "Think of what you want to imbue the blade with. Consider its purpose. The reason you gave it life."

Eggar thought of the tanner's daughter, his family, and the village that depended on him. He thought of the endless bandit demands, the constant fear of attack. He thought of the Lord in charge of the region, sitting comfortably in his lavish home far away, unconcerned with their plight. He thought about the long but satisfying day shaping the blade that would bring safety and security to those he loved.

"Now comes the tricky part," the stranger said. "Move the energy from the prisoner to the blade, but do not lose sight of the intention."

As the stranger spoke, Eggar felt the energy move from the man to the blade through him. He pictured a blade so sharp it could cut through all manner of materials, so strong nothing could harm it. A blade forged from beautiful moonlight, cold and crisp as a winter's night. As he pictured it, the energy entering the blade molded his thoughts into reality. The flow grew in intensity until it threatened to overwhelm him, but he clung to the image of the moonlight blade. He could feel the mark of every hammer fall, of every pass of the grinding stone. As he felt them, the energy refined each minuscule mark, perfecting it beyond possibility. There was no longer a barrier between the vision in his mind and reality. The feeling was exhilarating and terrifying in equal measure.

"It is almost done," the stranger added from far away. "Now you need to loop the energy into itself. Let me show you the pattern."

Inside Eggar's mind, an unfathomably complex pattern of glowing strands emerged. He did not understand it in the least, but he could feel it move from his mind into the blade. The energy from the prisoner dwindled into nothing as the pattern burned to life inside the blade, flowing in endless loops and swirls in perfect harmony.

He opened his eyes and felt tears streak down his face, born from the beauty he had witnessed. The room around him was only his familiar shop. He no longer felt like he was brimming with foreign energy, but some remnants of the magic remained inside him. The stranger's magic had opened something in his mind, but that door had not shut all the way when it left.

"I still feel funny," he said to the stranger as he sat heavily on the bench.

"A side effect of the process I assume," the stranger said with an uncomfortable look in his eyes. "If you ignore it, it will fade away in the next few days."

"That's good," Eggar said.

Despite his words, he wondered what would happen if he didn't ignore it. He wondered what kind of metalwork he could make if it stayed...

"You seem quite spent," the stranger said, his eyes returning to their unreadable but penetrating state. "Will you be able to fit the blade to the handle tonight?"

"I should," the smith said. "It's a simple task that I have done hundreds of times. For the most part, I have what I need in stock. I can work on a more permanent fitting over the next few days."

"Excellent news," the stranger said happily. "I shall return what remains of the prisoner while you attend to your work here."

"You won't need help?" Eggar asked, glancing at the prisoner.

It was odd to see the man just lying there, so still and quiet now. He knew he was dead, he could feel the emptiness in him, but he merely looked asleep.

"I can manage now that we don't have to keep him quiet," the stranger said as he unceremoniously lifted the corpse over his shoulder. "I need to be moving on at first light, so this will more than likely be goodbye. I hope that blade serves you and yours well."

"That's it? You will not wait to see the finished product?" Eggar asked, taken aback at the stranger's sudden exit.

"I would love to see it fully assembled, but I have tarried here as long as I can," he said sadly. "Who knows, perhaps we will meet again one day and you can tell me a tale of defeated bandits as well."

"Safe travels then, I suppose," Eggar replied with a weary smile.

The stranger nodded, smiled back, and then left as was his custom. The shop felt strangely empty and quiet after such a bizarre day. His eyes fell upon the blade lying on the workbench for the first time since the enchantment and what he saw made his breath catch. It was beautiful before, but now it was a flawless gem. He gently ran a finger down the body of the blade and felt the energy flowing inside. Oddly, he thought he could also feel the wealthy man's presence with him as well. The presence felt sad for its lost life, but there was also a deep sense of kindness. Perhaps it was his spirit come to thank him for avenging him. More likely, it was lack of sleep and his magic-addled mind playing tricks on him.

He turned away from the blade and fetched the materials he needed for the handle. He would finish the blade then go home and sleep for as long as he could. The world would make sense once more then.

CHAPTER 6

A Friend in Need

An urgent knock on the door jolted Eggar awake at his work bench, sore and disoriented. Before him lay the finished scythe, accompanied by a dark spot of drool where he'd passed out. His head and back ached, but sadly this was not the first time he'd woken up so. The knock sounded again, louder, urging him out of his seat. With a groan, he opened the door for an impatient young man.

"Yes?" Eggar asked, his tone shorter than he intended.

"I have come with an urgent message from the merchant," the boy said uncomfortably. "A wheel pin on his cart is broken and he is stranded a half day's ride from town on the main road. He cannot leave his goods and fears bandits may set upon him without help. He requests your aid with repairs right away and says he will pay you handsomely for the work."

"I'll see to it right away," Eggar said. "Would you do me a favor while I prepare to leave?"

The young man nodded sharply in reply.

"I need you to inform my wife what has happened. Ask one of the villagers how to get to my house, just about anyone can point the way for you."

"No need, the merchant told me where it is in case you were not in the shop."

"Clever," Eggar said as the sleep slowly burned away in his mind. "When you're done, stop by the inn for a good meal and a pint. Tell the barman I will settle your debt when I return."

"I appreciate the offer, but it is not necessary, sir. My da' says us country folk need to watch out for each other in times like these."

Eggar nodded appreciatively, impressed by the young man's sense of duty.

"Also, the merchant already paid me handsomely for the message," he added with a wry smile.

Eggar gave a surprised laugh. "Your honesty should be rewarded with a pint or two then, on me. Go, give my wife the news, you scamp."

"Yes sir!" The young man said with a smile then ran down the hill.

"If I still had that kind of energy," Eggar muttered to himself as he turned back into the shop for his tools and a new wheel pin.

Just before he headed out, a thump against his leg reminded him of the brooch in his pocket. He stashed it in his hiding spot, then returned to the main shop. He looked at the scythe for a moment, inspecting the makeshift trigger lever he'd attached last night. It was clunky and far from his best work, but it was sturdy and functional.

He considered the merchant's fear of bandits, then decided to take it with him just in case. He scooped it up along with his tool bag and locked up the shop. The sun was up, but the morning chill lingered, so it was early. He would borrow a horse from the innkeeper and ride to meet the merchant. They had a standing arrangement for such matters, each probably feeling like they got more from the bargain than they paid. Once the sun rose some and if the weather held, it should be a pleasant day for a ride.

The sun was high in the sky by the time Eggar saw the merchant's cart beside the road. The portly man lounged against a large sack of grain in the back of his cart as he stared at the clouds. The merchant's horse, happily grazing while tethered to the cart, noticed his arrival. Eggar smiled at the thought of how distraught the merchant sounded in his message, but here he was suffering more of boredom than bandits. The long haft of the scythe strapped to his back bumped against him and his own fears of being accosted tarnished his amusement.

"Hail fellow!" He called, which nearly startled the merchant into an early grave.

"Oh, Eggar! I am glad to see your friendly face!" the merchant said as he laboriously climbed out of his cart. "I thought for sure that young lad had taken my coin and left me to my fate."

"No, the good lad found me early this morning," Eggar said as he dismounted his horse. "How long have you been stranded out here?"

"Since yesterday evening. I had thought to leave your village early and make it to a comfortable bed in a particularly favorite inn of mine, but alas," he said, motioning towards the severed wheel. "I did have the good fortune of meeting that young man by chance shortly after the incident. I'm certain that if I had left my wares unattended to ride for help, I would have returned to an empty cart at best."

"Good fortune indeed," Eggar said as he inspected the wheel.

The pin was old and worn, but easily replaced. The job would require a strong back, but would not be difficult otherwise.

"Any sign of trouble?" he asked as he unpacked his tools.

"No, thankfully," the merchant said, watching. "Other than the young lad, I have only seen a group of the Lord's soldiers ride through. I asked them for help as well, but of course there was little they could do. They were urgently looking for someone lost in the countryside or something, but did promise to send help from the next town when they rode through."

"Nice of them," the smith said with a grunt as he positioned the wheel back on the axel.

The angle of the road and the cart worked in his favor and would have been nearly impossible by himself if it had been the other side. Even if they unloaded all the merchant's wares.

"Of course, I made the effort worth their while. To ensure the urgency of my situation remained at the forefront of their concerns," the merchant said.

"Of course," he agreed with a grin.

Eggar worked while the merchant prattled on and watched, but the road remained empty and quiet. By the time the new pin was hammered in place and the cart dug out, it was afternoon. He inspected the sky as he wiped a film of sweat from his dirty brow, gauging whether he could make it back home safely before dark. If he left right away and made good time, it would be close. On the other hand, he did not look forward to the prospect of a hard ride after his labors and a nearly sleepless night.

"Is it worthy to travel again?" the merchant asked.

"Better than before," Eggar said, showing him the old travel worn pin. "You should really have the others replaced soon though, if this one is any indication."

"I will do just that," the merchant replied jovially. "The day grows late, you are more than welcome to share my camp tonight. Unless you need to get home and are willing to brave the ride back."

"A tempting offer," Eggar said, considering it.

"I know how to cook a fine meal over a fire and have a cask of a particularly delectable red wine I'd planned on opening, if that makes any difference," the merchant said casually.

Eggar couldn't fault him for wanting company after spending a day and night staring at an empty sky. The thought of a good meal and friendly conversation was just as tempting for himself, truth be told. The journey home was a risk, albeit a minor one, but if he stayed they would both be safer for it.

"How could I turn down such a generous offer?" Eggar finally said.

"Excellent news!" his friend replied, overjoyed at the decision.

The two made camp beside the road and talked as old friends do until the sun went down while thier horses kept each other company nearby. The food, wine, and crackling fire eventually took it's toll and fatigue came upon him like a wave. He tucked the folded scythe close to his side and leaned back against the sack of grain that would be his pillow for the night.

"What is that you have been clutching this evening?" the merchant asked from across the fire.

"Ah, it is a new design for a scythe I finished last night. I thought to bring it with me in case I ran into brigands on the road," he explained with a yawn.

"I am not sure how effective a garden tool would be in a fight against the likes of them, but certainly better than nothing," the portly man said with an appreciative tone. "May I see it? I never tire of gawking at your craftsmanship."

"Certainly," Eggar replied, happy to show off his work. "The blade can fold with the use of the trigger on the handle here," he said, demonstrating how to use it by unfolding the blade.

The light blue metal glittered magically in the flickering firelight, more beautiful than he remembered. The merchant stared open mouthed for a moment before slowly reaching out to take it.

"Eggar, this is unlike anything I've seen you make before," he said as he marveled at the metal. "That is no trivial thing, mind you."

"Be careful, it is fiercely sharp," Eggar warned as the merchant gently ran a finger down the back of the blade.

"I have no doubt," he said, lost in his thoughts. "What is it made of? It is far lighter than I imagined it would be."

"It's an alloy made from those strange rocks you sold me," the smith replied with a proud smile.

"No!" the merchant said with pride and awe. "Did you use your furnace to make it?"

Eggar nodded happily. "I'll need to repair it before it can be fired again, but yes."

"Oh, that is fantastic news, dear friend!" the merchant said excitedly, then passed the scythe back to him to fold. "I am wondrously happy for you. No wonder you keep it so close. A blade that magnificent *and* the child of a lifetime's achievement?" The merchant pretended to swoon into his own bag of grain which made Eggar laugh. "Let us toast to your skills my friend."

"One more cup of wine, then I must insist on sleep," Eggar said, his fatigue beckoning once more.

"A finer idea has never been thought," the merchant said as he poured.

CHAPTER 7

Home

Despite a night spent on the hard ground, Eggar was in a fine mood as he rode toward home. After such trying days, the peaceful emptiness of the countryside had done him wonders. The wine, food, and exhaustion had made for wonderfully sound sleep. The hearty breakfast the merchant served hadn't hurt his spirits either. The sky was a marvelous shade of blue and nearly empty of clouds. He had passed two groups of travelers on the road, but each reported nothing but peace about the countryside. It seemed the Lord's soldiers were out in force looking for someone, which was enough to send the bandits into hiding. They would inevitably return, but he was thankful for any respite after such tragedy.

He was lost in thought as he rounded the mountainside that nestled his quaint little village. The scythe bumped against his back and the spare pins jingled happily against his saddle, tucked away in the tool bag. For some reason, his mind turned again and again to thoughts of the wealthy man that bought the brooch. He felt as though the man rode beside him, sharing the warm sunshine and fresh air in comfortable silence. A light breeze caressed his face, bringing with it the smell of last night's campfire from his clothes. It struck him as strange the smell lingered still, so he sniffed at the air with more focus. The smell was stronger, and did not smell like a regular fire. The stranger had mentioned the soldiers at the old garrison moving out soon, perhaps they were burning trash before leaving.

The farther around the bend he traveled, the stronger the smell of smoke grew. A knot began to form in his stomach, but he ignored it. The presence of the wealthy man touched his mind again, this time tainted with concern. He pushed the thought from his mind, feeling foolish and annoyed. Even so, he nudged his horse into a canter. Before he could see the village, the smell of smoke tickled his throat and a haze filled the air. He kicked the horse into a run, fear telling him something awful had happened in his absence. When he rounded the final turn, he pulled the horse to a stop, his mouth open in horror at what lay before him.

A thick column of black smoke rose from the village, billowing high into the sky. A house on the edge of town, barely visible from his position, had been reduced to smoldering rubble. Someone had attacked the village, but hopefully it was only the outskirts. He kicked the horse into a run, desperate for news. The closer he rode to town, the worse the scene became. Building after building lay burned out and destroyed. There were no other signs of violence, but also no people. His heart raced in time with the horse's hooves.

He stopped again when he reached the main road that ran through town. He nearly fell as he leaped from the horse's back, then retched in the street. The villagers must have tried to rally in the center of town, seeking safety in numbers but to no avail. Someone had began to pile the bodies, but left many lying in the street where they fell. Nothing moved among the smoldering buildings. Nothing lived. Eggar steeled his thoughts against the carnage and climbed back on the horse, his mind locked on his family. He prayed their little home had remained hidden away at the far end of town, untouched and forgotten. He needed it to.

The thick fog of smoke burned his lungs and stung his eyes as he rode, but he hardly noticed. His home rose from the high grass to meet him, but instead of the usual comfort he found only despair. He climbed from his horse, his body and mind numb as he took in the burned wreckage that was once his home. There was nothing left but a scorched shell. He fell to his knees in the dirt and wept at the sight. He could not understand what his eyes told him, what *all* of his senses told him. This could not be real. It had to be some sort of nightmare or illusion. He sat and freely wept for ages until the entirety of his soul felt hollow.

He finally stood as his eyes stared at the rubble without seeing it. His body was numb and his mouth dry, the smell of smoke everywhere. In his nose, on his clothes, coating his skin. He knew he should go inside, to confirm the fate of his wife and children, but the thought brought such pain that he could not. He knew what he would find and didn't have the strength to do it. Instead, he turned his back, ashamed of his weakness.

The horse had wandered off (an action he did not begrudge) so he walked down the high grass road back into town. He did not know where to go or what he would do, but merely followed his feet.

"You there! Halt!" a commanding voice yelled, drawing the smith's attention.

Before him stood three mounted soldiers in full armor that inspected him with hard faces. He had not heard them approach and wondered if they'd said something before. It hardly mattered.

"Who are you and what do you do here?" one soldier asked, his voice rough and angry.

Eggar stared back dumbly, unable to process the question, let alone answer.

"I asked you who you are!" the soldier yelled as he reached for his sword.

"I am the smith," Eggar said absently, the words more habit than thought.

"What hand did you have in this?" the soldier demanded.

"In what?" Eggar asked as his mind slowly engaged.

"Rebellion, what else?" another soldier asked, incredulous.

"What rebellion?" Eggar asked, confused. "What has happened here?"

"How is it you do not know?" the third soldier asked, calmer than the others. His armor was finer than the other two, suggesting he was some sort of officer.

"I have just returned from fixing a cart out of town, and my village is destroyed," he explained.

"The Lord's son came to this village only days ago and never returned," the officer explained. "He came to retrieve a brooch for his wedding, one you were meant to craft."

"The Lord's son? I made the brooch and he picked it up, though I did not know he was the Lord's son," Eggar said, distantly surprised. "I warned him to be careful of bandits. They were in town that day and would harm him if they thought there might be coin in it."

"Were you in league with the bandits that took him?" the first soldier asked hotly.

"Of course not!" Eggar said as his temper cut through the fog in his mind.

"Then how did the bandits know who he was?" the soldier shot back.

"How would I have told them? *I* did not know who he was!" Eggar said as anger burned in his chest.

"So you say," the second soldier added.

"Enough," the officer said to his men, then returned his attention to Eggar. "The Lord became worried when he did not return as scheduled and dispatched a host to find him, which we have been trying to do for several days. Yesterday, we received word from a messenger that the Lord had been set upon by bandits and terribly beaten, but would live. He was being treated in the old garrison where he could be easily defended until we could fetch him."

"No, he-" Eggar started, but was cut off.

"As we approached, we came across a man fleeing the town claiming the townspeople had joined forces with a band of brigands and were in open revolt. He said they had gone mad and had taken the Lord's son hostage," the soldier continued. "We came upon the garrison first and found the soldiers slaughtered and the Lord's son murdered in his room. The kitchen knife used was left on the floor in plain view."

"That cannot be!" Eggar exclaimed. "Why would we do such a thing? We have been petitioning the Lord for help with the bandits for months!"

"Perhaps you grew tired of waiting," the first soldier accused.

"You would do well to keep your mouth shut!" Eggar replied, his anger brimming.

"Enough, the both of you!" the officer shouted with authority. "Our commander will want to speak with you, whatever the situation may be. You will accompany us," he said as he climbed down from his horse.

Eggar continued to stare down the first soldier with a hot gaze, but did not plan to resist. Something nefarious was at work and the commander would have more information. Hopefully he would also be more willing to listen to reason. As the officer approached to take him into custody, the sound of beating hooves drew everyone's attention. A fourth mounted soldier skidded to a halt behind them and immediately addressed the dismounted man.

"Sir," he said crisply. "I was searching the smithy and found this secreted inside," he said as he held the silver brooch out for all to see. "It matches the one the Lord's son was to pick up."

"I told you he was in league with the bandits!" the first soldier said before the officer could reply.

Without hesitation, the soldier goaded his horse toward Eggar and drew his sword.

"Stop!" the officer yelled, but was ignored.

Something took control of Eggar's body and pulled the scythe from his back where it had been forgotten until now. In a fluid movement, he sidestepped the soldier's sword and countered with a heavy strike with the closed weapon. Caught unaware, the rider lost his balanced and rolled off the back of the horse. The second soldier was already on the move, surprised but ready to come to his compatriot's aid.

Eggar struck again and the blunt end of the scythe caught the oncoming soldier square in the breastplate, sending him off balance before his sword cleared the scabbard. The scythe spun around and hooked under the soldier's knee, then leveraged him off the far side of his horse where he struck the ground with a pained grunt. Eggar could feel the first soldier climbing to his feet behind him, still half dazed from the impact. The foreign energy inside him released the blade of the scythe and swung fluidly toward the man at his back.

Fully extended, the long curved blade easily covered the distance and the soldier fell on his backside to avoid it. The exposed blade glinted fiercely in the sun and the energy within Eggar surged in response, alien and yet intimately familiar. He recognized it as the spirit of the Lord's son that had been following him.

With sudden clarity, the truth hit him like a wave. The soldier had spoken the truth about the man at the garrison. It hadn't been a bandit, but the Lord's son! The bandits never stole the brooch because they'd never found it. He wasn't being visited by the man's ghost in thanks for avenging him, he'd was being haunted by the man he murdered and whose soul he'd trapped in the blade.

"What have I done?" he asked the empty air as his swing turned into another, then a third. "Why do you protect me so?" he desperately asked the imprisoned soul.

The soldier on the ground scrambled backward through the dirt to avoid the terrifying weapon wielded by a madman. Eggar's body shifted as the next swing reversed direction and caught the second soldier by surprise. The man yelped as the tip of the blade cleaved through his armor unchallenged, slicing through forged steel and thick leather strapping alike. The soldier stumbled backwards as his sword dropped from his hand and he clutched his chest. His pauldron hung loose, partially severed.

"Why do you defend me?" Eggar cried, desperate for an answer. "If it were not for me, you would still live!"

He felt the soul smile kindly at him as the feeling flowed from his hands into his mind. There was sadness and grief in the sensation, but more than anything there was forgiveness.

"I do not deserve this," Eggar said as tears filled his eyes. "Not for what I did to you."

Behind him, he heard the scrape of metal as the first soldier retrieved his blade and charged, undoubtedly hoping to catch him off guard. The forgiving soul inside the blade took control again and countered. The soldier tried to parry with his sword, but the blade of the scythe clipped straight through his weapon with a sharp click. The man's eyes were round in shock as the scythe rounded on him a second time, the gap much smaller. Escape from the blade's reach was impossible. He could only dodge, but his shock rooted him in place. The soldier and Eggar watched in equal horror as doom rended the air, the cutting edge of death hungry for the soldier's neck. The blade stopped a hair's width short. A pitiful whimper escaped the terrified man, his body rigid.

"Stand down!" the officer thundered behind Eggar. "You are no stranger to combat, that is for sure. You are no brigand though, as I would recognize the fighting style of the honor guard anywhere. Where did you learn such skills?" the officer asked, safely beside his horse.

"I do not know," Eggar said as he silently wished this whole nightmare would simply go away. "I am a smith, and a father. That's all I ever wanted, and now I am neither."

"You do not seem like you want to hurt anybody," the officer said gently. "Are you injured Benjamin?"

The second soldier's pauldron clinked as he moved his hand cautiously. Eggar saw the bright red blood that stained his fingers. Blood he had shed.

"No, sir. Only a scratch," Benjamin said stiffly.

"Too much blood has been shed this day already, good sir. Will you come with us to meet our commander? We can discuss what happened here and figure this out together." The officer's voice was gentle, but the tense undertone was unmistakable. "I think that's something we both want."

"What I *want* is my family," Eggar said through clenched teeth.

He tightened his grip on the scythe and the soldier at the other end flinched.

"Can you give me back my wife? Can you bring my children back from the dead?"

"I cannot," the officer said, the sadness in his voice genuine. "Nor could you do the same for that man's wife."

Eggar's grip softened as he noticed the tears in the soldier's eyes. The man's death would solve nothing, only add to the stain on his soul.

"What I want..." Eggar said, weary beyond words. "I want you to leave my village and never return. This land belongs to no Lord now save the angel of death. The living are no longer welcome here."

Eggar lowered the blade from the soldier's neck. The man considered retaliating, but then thought better of it. Instead, he edged around the smith as each kept a close eye on the other. Thick chains of grief pulled Eggar's body toward the earth, but he remained alert as the soldiers cautiously retreated to their officer's side.

"Leave this place, and never return," Eggar commanded tiredly and closed the blade with a snick.

The officer looked at him for a long moment and considered his options. Unwilling to risk his men further, he signaled them to depart. The fourth kept a close watch on Eggar as the other three mounted up. From above, the officer considered the victorious yet beaten smith for a very long moment.

"Come with us. There is nothing for you here," the officer said, his voice not commanding but compassionate.

"No," Eggar said flatly as he leaned heavily on the closed scythe.

The officer sighed, then glanced at his men, the silent order clear. As one, they turned their horses and left at a gallop. Eggar knew what would happen next. They would ride straight for the commander to report. Immediately after, the commander would put together a heavily armed force and ride for the village. They would return to either capture or kill him. He knew this, but none of it mattered. There was nothing they could do to him now that had not already been done. Death would be a relief, not a punishment.

CHAPTER 8

Dark Purpose

Eggar stood in the sanctuary of the tall grass for what felt like ages. Eventually, the stillness and silence threatened to crush him, so he walked. He had no destination, his only thought was to move in order to focus on something. Anything. Eventually, he climbed the hill to the smithy, guided by the force of habit. The familiar building, his life's work, was a ruin. Burned to rubble. With nothing better to do, he sifted through the wreckage and cleared debris. The building was gone, but the forge and his tools remained. Being born of fire, they were immune to the damage of a lesser flame. Dirty and smelling of ash and wood smoke, Eggar leaned on the forge and fought the fresh wave of nausea from his loss.

"It seems things did not turn out the way you expected," a voice said, which gave the smith an awful start.

Eggar spun, nearly losing his balance as he did. The cloaked stranger stood comfortably in the sun and observed him from a distance.

"You?" Eggar asked, his voice distant as his mind tried to comprehend what he saw. "You left town."

"And miss all this?" the stranger said as he turned to inspect the ruined village. "I simply could not leave without seeing the fruits of your labor. Quite the disaster," he said with a merry voice as he turned his gaze back to Eggar.

"You knew this would happen?" the smith asked as something in him shifted. "You did this on purpose."

"Me?" the stranger asked, incredulous. "Oh, this was all *your* doing! I simply gave you the tools."

"You tricked me," Eggar said, his voice hard.

"I didn't need to," the stranger replied. "Your kind does not need to be tricked. Given an ounce of power, it is your nature to destroy yourselves."

"No, it was you who convinced me to make this infernal blade!" Eggar yelled.

"Do not lay the consequences of your actions at my feet!" the stranger shot back. "I gave you the opportunity, that is all. Several times you questioned your course and I did *nothing* to sway you. You could have changed your mind a dozen times, but instead, you chose this. This is *your* doing, not mine!"

"I did not know this would happen," Eggar said as his voice quivered with rage.

"Didn't you?" the stranger asked as he took a step forward. "When did a weapon ever bring peace? You told yourself that the blade was for protection, but you wanted revenge for the tanner, didn't you? Weapons are made to bring death. Do not try to convince yourself otherwise."

"Why would you do this to us? What ill will do have for this village that you would do all this?" Eggar asked as he waved a hand toward the column of smoke that rose from the ruins.

"You?" the stranger asked, then laughed in his face. "You and your village are too insignificant to care about. You were merely the tools to make a point."

"To who? The Lord? The King?" Eggar asked.

The stranger laughed merrily. "You humans, you're so conceited. Ants playing at being God. My message is to the angels, you fool! They think you are so special, but I know the truth. Your existence is unnatural, an abomination. You are stitched together from unbalance and chaos, a stain that will spread unless it is scrubbed from existence."

"You murdered an entire village," Eggar started, but had to pause to clear the fury that blocked his throat. "You murdered my *family*, all to prove a point? To *angels*?" Eggar's voice had dropped to just above a whisper.

"Haven't you been listening, *friend?*" the stranger spat. "I did not murder anyone. *You* did."

Eggar's grief disappeared beneath the ocean of his fury, his body and soul aligned in perfect harmony for a single task. The stranger's words had left no doubt, no question, no indecision. He pressed the trigger and the blade of the scythe clicked into position, the soul inside in complete agreement with his intention.

"Your days of making points are done," Eggar said, his voice and eyes hard as the steel he forged.

Before the stranger could flinch, the blade of the scythe had pierced his chest and protruded from his back, slick with blood. His eyes were wide in disbelief and his mouth hung open as crimson death spilled over his lips in a fine line. Eggar stared into his eyes as the light faded from them. He removed the blade with a sideways jerk that nearly rended the man in two. The stranger's body hit the ground heavily and his eyes stared lifelessly into the sky.

Eggar stared at the corpse for a moment. He waited for the horror of what he'd done to hit him, but nothing came. No sensation filled his mind at all, only a strange numbness. He wiped the blade on the man's ruined cloak, then folded it and returned to his ruined workshop. Once again, his mind turned to what he would do next. The practical part of him said to pack what he could and wander the earth until he found a new town to settle in. Maybe travel to another land where nobody knew his face and start again. The thought felt wrong though. There were too many memories to leave behind here, both good and bad. The other part of him wanted to sit in the ruins of his workshop until he either starved to death or the soldiers returned to kill him.

"You'll not be rid of me that easily, smith," an impossibly familiar voice said behind him.

Eggar turned slowly, but could not comprehend the sight that met his eyes. There the stranger stood, alive. He brushed the dust from his cloak as if nothing had happened. The garment was stained with his blood and hung open on one side, yet the flesh beneath was pale and unmarred. The stranger met his eyes and smiled.

"How?" Eggar asked, dumbfounded.

"That blade of yours may be powerful, but not nearly powerful enough to end me," he said joyfully. "I am surprised at your willingness to try, though. I honestly didn't think you had the capacity for such violence."

Eggar's mind reeled as he glanced at the scythe and silently considered trying again.

"Go ahead," the stranger said and held his arms open. "Strike me down as often as you like. You will die of old age before I do from your blade. I'm afraid your vengeance will have to wait, however. You will need to use that blade on someone else first."

"What are you talking about?" Eggar asked as he pushed aside thoughts of murder.

If the first strike didn't kill him, there was no reason to believe the next would.

"The soldiers you so kindly let escape are riding back to their commander as we speak."

"What of it?" Eggar asked, annoyed.

"What do you suppose is going to happen when they get there?" the stranger asked tauntingly.

"They will report to their commander and he will send a host to either retrieve or kill me," Eggar said, his face flat.

"Not entirely the fool, I see," the stranger muttered. "What do you suppose will happen after that?"

Eggar stared at him defiantly, sick of his condescending attitude and mind games.

"The story of a blade so powerful a country smith could defeat trained soldiers will spread. The stories will be exaggerated into legend, and then Lords and peasants alike will seek to wield such power. Wars will be fought and the tragedy that visited your beloved little village will repeat over and over, never ending."

To Eggar's horror, he could see the truth in the stranger's words. As soon as word got out, the violent and powerless alike would be drawn to his creation like moths to a flame.

"You do have one hope," the stranger offered.

His face appeared serious and concerned, but Eggar could see the truth beneath it now. Beneath the perceptive eyes, he recognized the clever cruelty of the mind behind them. Everything his eyes gathered was fuel to torture what stood before him. Everything about him was a carefully calculated ruse built to deceive and destroy. Sermons about the insidiousness of the devil had not disturbed him, but this man made his skin crawl.

"What would you suggest I do, trickster?" Eggar asked, his disgust clear.

"Your only hope is to ride down the soldiers and end them before they make it back," the stranger said. "If you can kill them in time, you could disappear with your blade and this whole incident will remain a mystery. Of course, you will eventually die and the blade will be found, but at least you could delay your legacy a while."

"I will not stain my hands with more blood to amuse you," Eggar said, his tone final.

"Suit yourself, but your hands are already dripping. More will follow if you don't."

"I'll destroy the blade then," Eggar said.

The stranger laughed. "Good luck with that, dear smith. I think you will find that blade to be quite indestructible. In any case, my point has been made and I truly care not what you decide from here out. Eventually, that blade will usher in an age of fear and death, then everyone will thank Eggar the Smith for their plight. Your name will become a legend, and all will curse it."

With a merry laugh, the stranger turned and walked away. He whistled a happy tune as he disappeared down the path.

The stranger had left, but his words echoed in Eggar's mind. The smith furiously searched for a way to thwart the insane traveler's plans. He would not ride down the soldiers, that was not an option. He could try to destroy the blade, but the traveler was probably correct that he would be unable to. There had to be something the stranger had not thought of, some path he could take... Perhaps he could simply flee with the blade to some remote land. The story would still spread and he would eventually be hunted down. Even if he hid the blade, it would eventually be found.

He stared at the scorched forge as he thought and an idea floated from the ruins. He was unsure if it was possible, but a small hope was better than none. He focused deep inside his mind and felt the kernel of power the stranger had given him. It burned like a tiny ember, barely noticeable but there. He did not know how long it would take the soldiers to report and regroup, but he would have a couple of days at least. He took a deep breath and steadied his will as he scanned over the ruined village. The stranger would not win this fight, and his

village would not die in vain. He would make sure
of that in the only way he could see how.

Vengence

Eggar cleared an area around the forge and, with some rummaging, found the last of the light blue metal left over from the blade. It was not enough for what he needed, but he could fold it in with some of the steel parts he'd fished from the wreckage and make it work. With a serviceable work area and enough raw material, he fueled the forge and brought the blackened beast to life.

The clarion song of metal on metal played throughout the day as he pursued his single-minded purpose. Every strike of the hot metal was a prayer to those who died for his mistakes. Every creak of the makeshift bellows sang of his need to avenge them. Not with death, but with the countless lives he would save. Time was a meaningless concept as he folded the metal and then hammered it out into the long shaft of its final shape. The sun fell and night came, but Eggar yet poured himself into his work leaving nothing in reserve. Hunger gnawed at his stomach but he did not eat. Sweat poured from his brow but he did not drink.

The staff reached its final form, but Eggar was not finished. With his set of now scorched and pitted awls, he sculpted fine details into the metal. He poured his sorrow and grief into the carvings, along with his loss, his anger, his guilt. He told the story of his life and his downfall without words. He doubted anybody would understand, but that did not matter. It was there.

As a final touch, he etched a warning in intricate script down the backside of the staff: "All who bear this blade shall feel the cold grip of death." He inspected his work, confident it was his best yet. As with every piece, he saw the lingering tiny flaws but to refine them away was beyond the skill of his mortal hands. It was not perfect, but nothing ever was. This would be his final and greatest work, and with that he was content.

As the weakness of his labors took hold of his body, he fit the trigger assembly and blade into the staff. They came together as if destiny had shaped them instead of his calloused hands. He tested the movement of the blade and nodded appreciatively when it was flawlessly smooth.

The soul inside the blade reached out and touched Eggar's mind with loving concern, aware as ever of his intentions.

"Do not worry for me, dear friend," Eggar said to the blade, unsure if the soul inside could hear him. "It is the only way I can stop the damage of my sins."

The soul of the Lord's son understood, but grieved for the smith nonetheless.

Eggar gazed at the pink and orange fire that spread through the sky from the setting sun one last time. Prepared, he cut his hand with a sharp piece of debris. Blood welled up from the wound, and he wiped it the length of the staff. He held the reforged scythe aloft as he reached into the ember of magic inside him and directed it into the staff. The magic flared to life, bright as flame, as he focused on the energy in the blood. To his surprise, the complex pattern the stranger had shown him remained in perfect detail, burned into his memory. As the pattern took shape in the staff, he perfected the design and filled it with his intentions. The purity of the metal felt different, but the magic remained the same. The sensation of the world around him grew dim. His hunger and thirst faded as the pattern solidified and pulsed with power. The weakness and pain in his limbs fell away to nothing. The world around him became a shadowed reflection, but he was no longer part of it. He floated, formless, in an empty void save for the soul of the Lord's son. Together, perhaps they could find a measure of peace here, untouchable by the world beyond.

CHAPTER 10

Wreckage

The commander marched up the hill in even strides despite his heavy armor. Beside him strode the officer in charge of the initial contact with the village. Behind them, the commander's squire led his horse accompanied by a foot soldier.

"I realize most of your men lack experience and you are somewhat new to command yourself, but you must keep better control of them," the commander chided. "There was no need for this situation to escalate as it did, nor should two of your men have been injured by a smith."

"Yes sir," the officer said crisply.

The group approached the ruined smithy and surveyed the damage.

"It seems we have found our renegade smith," the commander said as he gazed into the ruins of the workshop. "As for your men," the commander said as he turned back to the officer. "The Lord would not be pleased to hear I had your men flogged for avenging his son. However, I can give them punishment details for disobeying their commanding officer. Gather your troops and have them bury every last one of the fallen villagers. Ensure the bodies are prepared with respect and laid to rest in proper graves with markers. If the graves are hastily dug, have them fill it in and start again. They will carve name plaques for any that can be named. They will work on half rations until they are finished and not a single soldier leaves this village until *every* fallen villager is cared for. Make it clear this is what happens when your command is disobeyed. If any refuse your orders, inform them I will personally flog them for disobeying mine, no matter the Lord's feelings about it."

"Yes sir," the officer said at attention.

"I'll not tell you how to organize your men for this task, but it may be best to give the two men that instigated the fight with the smith the worst of the detail," the commander added, his voice softer.

"I had already planned on making an example of them, sir," the officer said grimly. "I hope this will provide a much-needed lesson in restraint for them both."

The commander gave a small smile, then curtly nodded his dismissal.

When the officer turned and marched off down the hill, the commander returned his gaze to the body in the ruined workshop once more.

"Let us comb through this rubble and see if we can divine some clues as to what the hell happened here," the commander said to the foot soldier.

The soldier nodded and the two of them climbed over fallen beams and charred debris. Slowly, they cleared a rudimentary path to the smith's body. The soldier turned the body over to search for a cause of death.

"He's been dead a while," the soldier said as the commander inspected the ruins around them.

"It looks like some of this was cleared already," the commander said, eyeing the anvil and forge.

"What were you doing up here?" he asked the empty air.

"Sir, I think I found the weapon," the soldier said as he held up the folded scythe.

Even with the blue blade tucked away into the black metal handle, it was a menacing sight.

"Be careful with that!" the commander warned. "Who knows what devilry is at work in a blade that can slice through armor."

The commander's eyes scanned the area around the body until they locked on an unburned wooden handle. It must have been brought here after the fire, but for what purpose he did not know. His brow furrowed in thought.

"What do you suppose this does," the soldier said, then pressed the trigger in the haft of the scythe.

The blade slid open with a click and the man screamed in pain. He tried to drop the weapon, but the skin of his hand had frozen to the handle. Frost rapidly formed along the staff and engulfed the poor soldier's fingers. The commander scooped up a scorched hammer from the rubble and came to the soldier's aid without hesitation. He used his gloved hand to carefully press the soldier's fingers back into the trigger and slid the blade shut with the hammer. The blade snapped shut with a click and the frost ceased its advance. The soldier continued to scream as his hand remained frozen to the metal.

"Hansel, bring water!" the commander called to his squire. "Hurry!"

The squire snatched the water skin from the saddle and clamored over the wreckage. The commander poured water over the soldier's hand which melted the ice and slowly freed his fingers.

"Easy, hold your hand still," he ordered as the soldier tried to pull his hand away. "Let me see."

The commander inspected the waxy texture of the flesh and the blue hue that had crept in. His hand had only been in contact with the scythe for seconds, but frostbite had already set in.

"It's bad, but you should recover," the commander said. "I've seen many such injuries fighting in the winter when men touch unprotected armor. Do not try to move your hand and have the healer wrap it tightly with clean bandages. Tell no one but the healer of what occurred here and ensure he knows to keep it to himself as well. He is notoriously discreet, but tell him nonetheless."

The commander helped the man up, then watched as his squire helped him through the wreckage. Once he was sure they were able to make it out, he returned his attention to the scythe. He removed the thick glove from one of his hands, then cautiously tapped the dark metal of the handle. His fingertip did not freeze to it, so he risked his hand. It was very cold, but no longer freezing.

"Is that wise sir?" his squire asked as he returned to his master's side.

"I believe it is only dangerous when opened," the commander said as he gently lifted it. "It is lighter than I expected."

He ran a finger down the spine of the closed blade, marveling at the cold blue metal. He turned it to gaze upon at the images of vines, flowers, bones, and skulls that made an elaborate pattern down the staff. The carvings were impossibly detailed and seemed significant, although the meaning eluded him. His eyes swept over the delicate lettering on the back of the staff and he smiled bitterly.

"Cold hand of death indeed," he muttered to himself. "Where on earth did you find this, smith?" he asked the corpse, but of course did not receive an answer. "See to it that this man is laid to rest with the others," he said to his squire without averting his gaze. "No matter his degree of responsibility in this tragedy, he deserves what little dignity there is in death."

"I will see to it," the squire said solemnly. "What of the weapon?"

"I shall take it with me, but we tell nobody," the commander said as he stood, the weapon in hand. "Inform any who heard the report that it was destroyed. Make sure the soldier and the healer both understand the wound was caused by a lump of hot coal in the forge and that no one may ever know of this weapon. When we return, we will find it a proper home where it can fade away into the obscurity of time."

The squire nodded, but a confused expression remained.

"If word gets out about such a weapon, people will come from around the world to try and claim it," the commander explained. "Many would be hurt or killed in the attempt, not to mention those that would be hurt *by* it. Heaven help us if someone is powerful enough to actually wield it."

"So we hide it away and hope it is forgotten," Hansel said.

"Or we find a better solution," the commander added. "Should we need to discuss it, we shall call it Halcyon. It will not bring happiness or peace in our hands, but if we can keep it out of others it may rest in it. Fetch me something to wrap it in to hide it from prying eyes, then we shall ride from the shadow of this place."

CHAPTER 11

The Steward's Legacy

A guard in full armor stood at attention and eyed the stranger before him with a wary gaze. The guard's hand rested on the hilt of his sword, fingers relaxed but ready. The stranger was wrapped in a dark black cloak, the hood drawn to throw inky shadows over his face. What little could be seen beneath the cowl was covered in an equally dark mask. Dark leather gloves covered the man's hands and black riding boots hid his legs and feet. The man was a shadow in the flesh with the exception of the long blonde braid that spilled from the hood and the piercing blue eyes that scanned the room.

Despite the stranger's mysterious dress, his stance was one of relaxed curiosity. He inspected the armory hall like a house guest. He gazed at the architecture and braziers and occasionally felt the stone of the wall. He had not spoken, only nodded to acknowledge the guard's presence as the commander had left him there. Footsteps ascended the stairs behind the guard and drew the stranger's attention, his gaze focused but body relaxed. The commander emerged from the shadowed stairs, a long cloth-wrapped bundle in his hands.

He was dressed in the cloth uniform worn by officers yet moved as if in armor, a testament to the many battles of his youth. His parchment skin bore the lines and folds of time and his hair had gone from dark brown to silver white. Despite his age, he retained the toned and scarred body of a career soldier.

The journey along the stairs grew slower with each passing year, but it had yet to defeat him. All the same, he was glad to pass his charge on to someone else, for more reasons than his knees.

"You have done our order many great services. I appreciate such aid more than I can express, sir," the commander said to the stranger. "Your ability as a warrior is unsurpassed by any I have seen, and I suspect that will remain true long after I am gone. I saw you fight in the gorge many years ago, you know."

"Ah," the stranger said as he gently shook his head. "That was a dark time indeed. Far too many souls departed there."

The commander sighed deeply, a sound full of grief and regret. "Far too many indeed," he said, his eyes focused on the past. "I saw you fight at the tip of the spear that broke their lines. You wore no armor and wielded a chipped sword, yet you emerged from that battle without injury." The commander shook his head, still in awe of the memory. "I have never seen a creature on God's earth do the things you can. That speech you gave when they dug into the caves... That drove fear into the bones of friend and foe alike."

The stranger chuckled and shuffled his feet. "I've found that a bit of showmanship can end most battles before they begin," he said.

"Well, it certainly did then," the commander said with a wry smile. "I've heard the men used to joke that they didn't surrender sooner because they soiled the first white flag and had to find another."

The guard suppressed a laugh and the stranger rubbed the back of his neck.

"Without your intervention, that day would have spun into a drawn-out war of attrition," the commander said, his expression grave. "For every life you took on the battlefield, you easily saved ten."

"Yet I still regret the ones taken," the stranger said softly, almost to himself.

"That was many years ago now, and I was a much younger man," the commander said. "I have grown old and yet you are untouched by the years."

"The mountain is unmoved by time, but not untouched," the stranger said cryptically. "At least that's what my father used to tell me. That was a very long time ago now," he said, his voice distant.

"I had many reservations about giving up my stewardship of this weapon," the commander said as he gazed upon the cloth-wrapped bundle. "However, your unmatched skill in combat, your reticence to take a life, and your enduring youth have done much to assuage them. If you are willing, I would like to pass the safekeeping of this to you."

The guard remained silent, but his eyes were fixed on the wrapped bundle. He had guarded this passage and its only connecting room for many years, but never knew what it was he kept watch over. This post had always been considered of dire importance by the commander, though he pretended it wasn't. The room was nothing special, only storage for dusty tomes and relics. He'd seen the bundle tucked away in a corner countless times, but never thought much of it. He'd suspected one of the books contained a grave secret or perhaps one of the odd items possessed some obscure value, but not once had he suspected the bundle of any worth. He'd assumed it was a broom or something that had been left behind by a careless servant and then forgotten.

"What is it?" the stranger asked.

"It is a weapon of incredible power. I feared it would be sought out and used to ill ends, so I and a few others secreted it away. Now I am the only one left alive who knows its history."

"May I?" the stranger asked and held out a gloved hand.

"I must warn you, the blade attacks any who open it with intense cold," the commander said as he gently handed it over.

"Interesting," the stranger said as he took the bundle.

He removed his gloves, the skin beneath pale and flawless, then unwrapped the scythe. He silently inspected it, running a finger over the carvings in the staff. The commander watched in silence, his expression intent but not tense.

"Where did it come from?" the stranger asked, his eyes still fixed on the weapon.

"I'm afraid that remains a mystery," the commander said. "The Lord's son was murdered in a small village not far from here and we had reports of a brewing insurrection. Everything spiraled out of control and the village was wiped out. I found the blade in the wreckage of the smith's shop, though how it found its way there I have no idea."

"This is unlike any blade I have seen," the stranger said as he inspected the spine of the retracted blue metal.

"I have not seen its like before either," the commander said. "There is some sort of magic about it as well, and I am not the sort to believe in that kind of thing." The commander frowned as he stared at the weapon. "I suspected for a time that it was cursed, as it turned up during a dark time for our land. The realm suffered from one crisis after another for many years after we found it, all seemingly without relation or cause. Then one day it all stopped and everything fell back into a quiet rhythm. I no longer consider it the blade's doing, but I cannot shake the feeling there is some connection. Some sinister force at work. Perhaps that is just wishful thinking, though. It would be much easier to understand if it were."

"I have found the minds of men are capable of being sinister enough without help," the stranger said as he briefly met the commander's eyes.

The commander grunted his agreement. "Be careful-" he started to warn as the stranger pushed the trigger to release the blade, but it was too late.

The blade swung open and clicked into place, then frost quickly grew around the stranger's fingers. Small crystals of ice traced their way along the intricate carvings in the staff, but the stranger only watched.

"Easy my friend, I am not your enemy," he said softly to the blade. "So much pain and guilt in you, be at peace."

The frost slowed to a stop, but the stranger's hand remained encased. The commander and guard watched in amazement as the stranger whispered to the blade to soothe its anger as if it were alive. As the frost receded, the stranger moved his fingers to shatter the ice that held them.

"Are you hurt?" the commander asked, taken aback.

"No, I am fine," the stranger said, a smile in his voice. "Cold has no effect on me, and it seems as though the blade and I have come to an... understanding. For now at least."

The stranger closed the blade and wrapped it back up. His hands moved quickly, but they handled it with the utmost respect. When finished, he replaced his gloves and nodded at the two men.

"I am honored to be its new guardian and you can be assured it will not leave my possession for as long as I live," the stranger said.

Thank you for reading!

I hope you enjoyed reading this as much as I enjoyed writing it.

If you happen to be reading this for free, I love that you got a chance to! Maybe you borrowed it, found it, or pirated it. I can't say that last one's okay, but I'm still glad you're here.

If you enjoyed it and want to help me keep writing more stories, I'd encourage you to check out my website for donation copies of my works. They're discounted electronic versions that help support my writing. Purchasing one is a great way to say thanks and let me know you want to see more. If you can't, no worries! I'm just glad you're here!

No matter what, you're awesome and thanks again for reading!

~Eugene Pendley

www.eugenependley.com/donations

"I am relieved to hear it. Where will you go?"

The stranger offered no answer save his silence.

"Well, wherever you go, I wish you the best of fortunes," the commander said, truly grateful. "I'm not sure it matters, but the few of us who knew about the blade named it Halcyon, in hopes it would either bring peace or, at least, not disturb it."

"It is a fine name," the stranger said and his tone suggested he knew something they did not.

He nodded his goodbye, then turned and strode away without a word. The two men watched as his cloak flowed behind him, out of the dim torchlight and into the shadows of time.

www.ingramcontent.com/pod-product-compliance
Lightning Source LLC
Chambersburg PA
CBHW071529100726
47908CB00004B/1331